A Bellsong
for
Sarah Raines

❧ ❧ ❧

BETTIE CANNON

CHARLES SCRIBNER'S SONS

NEW YORK

Chapters 26 and 27 were published in slightly different form, under the title "The Rainesingers," in *The Journal for Kentucky Studies*, vol. 2, September 1985.

Excerpts from lyrics of *All Alone* by Irving Berlin on page 70:
   © Copyright 1924 Irving Berlin
   © Copyright renewed 1951 Irving Berlin
Reprinted by permission of Irving Berlin Music Corporation.

Charles Scribner's Sons Books for Young Readers
Macmillan Publishing Company
866 Third Avenue, New York, NY 10022
Collier Macmillan Canada, Inc.

Printed in the United States of America
First Edition   10 9 8 7 6 5 4 3 2 1

Library of Congress Cataloging-in-Publication Data
Cannon, Bettie Waddell.   A bellsong for Sarah Raines.
   Summary: Surrounded by the warmth of new-found relatives and friends in a small Kentucky town, fourteen-year-old Sarah is eased of the sadness of her father's suicide in Detroit during the Depression and finds a way to celebrate his life.
   [1. Fathers and daughters—Fiction.   2. Suicide—Fiction. 3. Kentucky—Fiction.   4. Depressions—1929—Fiction]   I. Title.
PZ7.C17138Be   1987   [Fic]   87-4299   ISBN 0-684-18839-2

For my husband, Chuck,
and for Charlie, Sallie, Kate and Sue

ACKNOWLEDGMENTS

Grateful acknowledgment is offered here to Eliot Wigginton and his students for their *Foxfire* books, numbers 1,2,3, and 7 (Anchor Press/Doubleday, New York), which helped me with mountain lore and language; to Barbara Neal and Joan Peters for their Depression memories; to cousins Datter and Charlotte Nolan, my Kentucky connection; to members of Detroit Women Writers, whose names would fill this page, for encouragement and prudent attention at readings and workshops; to Elizabeth Buzzelli, Ann Hellie, and Cynthia King, for editorial advice; to Sue Hudson, Iris Byrne, and Eleanor Mooney, for typing. Special thanks to Clare Costello, editor, for her gentle persuasions and her faith, and to Iris Jones, Cecelia Himes, and my sister, Esther Waddell Mohan, who always knew this bellsong would come to life.

1

Sarah Raines opened her eyes to find Uncle Marshall Stannard, Mama's brother, standing in her room in the morning's half light. She had met him for the first time only three days before at the funeral, and now here he was, taking over her life. And Mama's life. Pretending that this was not the day she had to leave home forever, Sarah curled herself up under the bedclothes and closed her eyes again.

"Time to rise and shine. It's four A.M.," he said. "Come on, honey."

Get out of my room was what she wanted to say. This room was hers, had been for all her fourteen years. Daddy called it her hidey-hole, away from all the troubles of the house. Now her room was different, changed like everything else. Boxes of Mama's old Greek and Latin texts, what was left of Grandmama's hand-painted dishes, and bushel baskets full of Daddy's clothes were stacked under the eaves. The antique furniture Uncle Marsh sent when Grandmama and Grandaddy died had been carried upstairs and pushed into corners with sheets draped over it. Mama wasn't going to leave anything good out where renters could use it. She would lock the door at the foot of the stairs and Sarah's attic room would be closed off for who knew how long.

"The big day is here, Sarah." Uncle Marsh put another box on the floor. "Your Mama said for you to get up. 'Now,' she said."

It was still dark. Birds called their first morning sounds to each other from across the street in the little park filled with trees and clumps of honeysuckle waiting for leaves and blooms. Sarah closed her eyes again.

The casket seemed to sink into the ground while everyone stood in the cemetery in the cold watching it go. Why didn't someone try to stop it? Maybe her father wasn't really inside that narrow wooden box with the black cloth tacked over it. Who had seen John Andrew placed inside? Why didn't Mama cry? Mr. Hackley, the minister Mama called in from Westbrook Methodist Church, spoke again in his rich, unaccented voice. "Dust thou art to dust returneth," he said, and then he said something more about how life dies each night and begins anew each morning like blossoms that fade. He said some more words about our reluctance to bridge the chasm of death. Sarah thought the greatest chasm she knew anything about was the perfectly rectangular hole in the earth into which John Andrew's coffin sank like water in sand. In what seemed an eternity of time, Mama fell, fell with her arms stretched out before her, fell without a word onto the snow-littered ground.

Sarah kept her eyes shut tight, trying to forget what she knew was true, but with Uncle Marsh standing next to her at four o'clock in the morning, how could she forget that today was the day she had to drive south from Detroit to Hanlon, Kentucky, to live with him. After they cleaned up for possible renters whom they might entice with low rent and rooms of furniture, Mama and Sarah would pile into Uncle Marsh's green Hupmobile with all their *lares et penates*, as Mama put it. Mama was going back where she was born, where she was Lucey Stannard, not Raines. Sarah was going to the ends of the earth, as far as she was concerned. Yes, they were on their way with Uncle Marsh to live in the big house Grandmama willed to him instead of Mama. That was because Mama married Daddy instead of some doctor's son the way Grandmama wanted her to do.

"You have to go live in a coal mining town to keep from going on the dole and taking welfare money the way all the poor people do," was what Nancy Pettibone, her best friend said. Sarah had seen the newspapers with headlines about unemployment and the thing her father's friends called the Depression. She was beginning to understand now why Janelle Rosa from school hid in the girl's bathroom during lunch period. Janelle didn't want people to know that she had only a cold, boiled potato smeared with grape jelly for her lunch each day, so she ate it hiding in the girl's lavatory, alone. There was no money for lunch, not since her father lost his job and they had to move out of the upper flat they rented down the street. Instead of moving to Kentucky, Janelle's big family had to crowd into rooms behind their family candy store up on Fullerton Avenue. Those hard times that everyone talked about quietly while listening to the news on the radio touched everyone, Sarah thought, but Janelle's father didn't . . . she couldn't think the word, not even to herself.

The heaviness began again, growing in her like bread rising in a bowl. She scrunched down in the bedclothes. Perhaps she would never waken again. She would die, like

Daddy. That was it. Then she wouldn't have to think about the terrible thing she had seen, the sounds she heard in the park across the street. She wouldn't have to think about going on the dole and having to stand in line for food and money, she wouldn't have to burn her baby crib and cupboard to keep warm. She wouldn't have to leave her little, low-ceilinged room, her place in the world.

She decided to make Uncle Marsh disappear. Maybe all the rest of it would go away, too. She held her breath and squinched up her eyes, contracted all the muscles in her body. She said a kind of queer prayer about turning back the days and beginning again. In a minute she would go downstairs and have oatmeal and brown sugar with Daddy. It would be summer and she'd walk with him up to the streetcar stop at the corner. She'd watch him board the yellow car with the other men. He'd lift his lunch bucket in a salute. She'd wave. . . .

No. Can't happen. It was Mama's voice in her head. Mama's practical voice. Sarah felt all the tears she would ever have waiting there behind her eyes. They would spill out and never stop if she wasn't more careful.

"Hey, you dreamin'? It's time to 'waken. Day's a-breakin'. Hoecake a-bakin'."

Uncle Marsh touched her eyelids with a soft touch. Sarah willed herself not to feel anything. *Why does he touch me in that feathery, mothery way? Daddy never did that. Never said cheerful, rhymey things, even when he was drinking too much whiskey. No, it was as if Daddy forgot everything except sadness.*

But she wasn't going to like Uncle Marsh. No. He was nothing but a kidnapper. She thought about Baby Lindbergh, whose father's fame hadn't saved him from being kid-

4

napped the year before and she wrote new fat headlines in her head.

UNCLE KIDNAPS NIECE!

Large, dark letters swam through her mind. *Fourteen Years Old. Forced to Live in Coal Mine. Taken From Friends Without Notice.*

Uncle Marsh did not disappear. She breathed in. She had to, finally, and she caught the smell of his cigarette and sweat and something else, a smell she couldn't name. She pretended it was her father, dark and running-board thin as she was, at the foot of the bed, not Uncle Marsh with his packing boxes and smiles. Daddy came into her room often at night. She saw him in the dark, silhouetted against the low windows, swaying gently, holding onto her bed or the door as if he were on a sailing ship. He'd smile too broadly with wet, bloodshot eyes, talking, talking, talking until Mama came upstairs in her bathrobe to lead him away, to stumble with him down the stairs while he mumbled words Sarah couldn't understand and would never forget. Though Mama never said a word about it, Sarah knew her father was drunk. Falling down dead drunk, was what Nancy said.

Uncle Marsh pointed toward the wall of boxes. "Your Mama said to fold up your bedclothes. Put 'em in that box. It's still open."

She sat up. Uncle Marsh started out the door and then turned back toward her. He ducked his head under the low eaves. Sarah fumbled with her hair, hair like black electric wires—"like mine," Daddy said, while Mama laughed and said, "More like Medusa, if you ask me."

"Sarah." Uncle Marsh's voice came out of the dimness. She couldn't look at him; both of them had such terrible secrets to bear. She couldn't look at him for fear he would know hers and she would know his. "I reckon this is mighty hard for you," he was saying. "You know though, don't you, you and Lucey . . . you and your mama cannot go on eatin' last year's canned tomatoes for breakfast, stealin' the electric company's electricity by tappin' in from the pole? How many Co'Cola bottles you think you can find to get the pennies?"

"I don't know. I was scared. Scared we'd get caught about the electricity. Mama didn't want me to. We burned my baby furniture. Grandmama gave it to me. We burned Daddy's . . . the workbench." She said the words before she could stop them. She hadn't wanted to talk to him. She still could not look at him, not at his face, his eyes. He touched her again with his slender hand.

"You helped as best you could, child. Now it's my turn."

He leaned down to kiss her. She felt his breath moist on her cheek, felt the warm closeness of his body, smelled talcum powder.

She wanted to tell him to *go on, get out of my room. Leave us alone. We will manage. We were, we could have done it.* But she could only stare at him just the way Mama told her not to. *Don't stare at him, Sarah. Whatever you do in this world, do not stare.*

It was the scar Mama didn't want Sarah to look at.

Flowing like fire down into his open shirt collar, red-ridged scars were laid over purplish skin like pie dough stuck to a smooth board. The purple skin was too slick and shiny, stretched across his chin, to be real. She felt sick but made herself look again at what Mama called his badge of bravery.

6

Mama said he got a medal for honor and courage when it happened in a French forest somewhere.

"This is some of what I carry as a reminder of the war to end all wars," he said. It was the war fought in Europe that ended the year before she was born. "You can look. You'll get used to it."

He seemed to pause, tilt his head, let her read all she wanted of the terrifying story on his face and neck. "It doesn't bother me. Not anymore." He said it as if he had said it to himself many times before this time.

When he arrived two days after Daddy died, Sarah had avoided him for fear she'd see what Mama had warned her about. At the funeral, she wouldn't sit close to him, sat with Nancy and her mother instead. But now she had to look. No matter what Mama said, she had to look at the scarred face illuminated by the streetlight.

"Once you get used to it, you can stand almost anything," he said. But Sarah didn't think that was true, not for her.

"Does it hurt?" was all she could think of to say.

"Not anymore. No." He lit another cigarette. His hands shook slightly.

Through the rising smoke, she saw his green eyes, too light for his face. Had flames from his own flesh burning risen past his eyes? Had he peered into the smoke back then, too, she wondered? How could he act now as if nothing had happened? She would never be like that. She would never forget her scars, the things that happened to her. Never.

"Well," he said, "let's go down. The big day is here."

❧ 2 ❧

Mama packed a picnic lunch to eat in the car, did up the breakfast dishes and packed them in the last pasteboard box. Uncle Marsh took the piece of ice left in the oaken icebox and threw it into the yard. Sarah, as she emptied the drip pan into Mama's roses for the last time, watched the ice melt in the grass.

"Oughtn't we to take it over to Mrs. Drisdon?" She stared at the glittering chunk of smooth ice.

Mama agreed it was a waste but didn't ask Sarah to walk across the driveway with it.

"Marshall," Mama said instead, "if you'd been around here trying to make ends meet after two pay cuts and no job for so long, you'd be a sight more careful. Use it up, wear it out, make it do, do without." Mama quoted the words that everyone repeated over and over to each other now that times were so bad.

"Lord have mercy, Lucey, that ice isn't enough to bother

with. It'll last about as long as you two could stayin' on here alone," Uncle Marsh said.

"We lasted as long as the coal held out, didn't we, Sarah?" Mama propped the icebox door open with a stick and pulled down another window blind.

"You didn't want to take any free coal from the man," Sarah said. "Not even three baskets."

"It was cannel coal, Marsh. We don't burn soft coal."

"Mama, it was better than nothing even if it does smoke things up when it burns. All we had to do was shovel it into the coal bin. The man was nice. . . ."

Mama smiled. "You should have seen her. Practically curtsied, fell all over herself thanking the *coal* man."

Sarah pictured the scene in her mind's eye. It was the week before Daddy died. The coal was gone and Mama didn't even know where Daddy was. He had been gone like that before, stayed away maybe two or three days at a time. Sarah never knew where he went. But Mama knew, all right. He'd come home each time full of remorse and burdensome kindnesses. But this time it was different. This time while he was gone, Mama found the letter in the front hall closet: the letter said John Andrew Raines was on indefinite layoff until further notice. They were sorry, they said. Clipped to that letter was a notice from the Federated Motors Company closing their place of business. The letters were six months old. Daddy didn't have pay cuts, the way he said. He didn't have any pay at all.

"But he went to work every day, Mama," Sarah had said.

"Yes."

"You packed him a lunch every single day."

"I know it. You walked him up to the streetcar stop, too."

He'd had no job at all for all this time. This meant, Mama said, that they'd lose the house. There wasn't any money coming in. The bank would take the house, foreclose on the mortgage.

They had stared at each other that day, Mama standing on a chair to reach the green box on the top shelf of the closet, Sarah looking up at her. Sarah couldn't imagine where Daddy hid himself on all those long days. Did he go to the library and read newspapers with their black headlines about hard times? Or stand in long lines to look for jobs? Maybe he went to blind pigs, those closed up, secret places where men like Daddy sat drinking whiskey out of silver-rimmed glasses. Sarah imagined ladies with low-cut dresses like movie stars seated at the Tables for Ladies and Daddy there, slim and sad, holding his cigarette between his thumb and forefinger the way he did.

Or did he eat Mama's lunches on a park bench with all the other men like those she'd seen in newsreels at the movies on Saturdays? Was he a member of the great army of unemployed FDR, President Roosevelt himself, talked about on the radio? If these things happened, why hadn't he told Mama or her? How could he have pretended that his life was one thing when it really was another? He'd gone on so long pretending, how did he know what was real? Is that why he wanted to die? Sarah didn't want to think about it all, but when Mama found the bankbook with a pattern of holes stamped through it saying that the account was closed, she had to think about it right along with Mama.

That night they had slept in Mama's and Daddy's big

bed, curled together like spoons while Mama sang, "Husha-bye, don't you cry. Go to sleepy, little baby." Mama sang to comfort herself, too, Sarah decided. Two days later Daddy came home, his bloody knees showing through torn trousers, a stubble beard on his face, his skin gray. When he learned what Mama had found in the closet, that his secret had been discovered, he exploded into that last terrible rage.

But Mama wasn't singing any lullabyes to Sarah now. Instead she hurried around the rooms, checking everything, taking more flotsam and jetsam, as Uncle Marsh put it, out to the car. Sarah hated the way their house looked now with tables bare, Mama's music gone from the piano, no bouquets of Mama's roses and those little flowers that looked like bells filling the air with fragrance. Sarah stood in the middle of the living room while Mama swept around her.

"Sarah. I hope," Mama said, "I hope you are not dawdling. Are you? I know you don't want to leave . . . Nancy and all, but. . . ."

Sudden tears filled Sarah's eyes. She stared down at her old-lady, navy blue leather shoes that Mama got free-for-the-taking from Mrs. Drisdon. Even though the oxfords were two sizes too big for her, Sarah had to wear them anyway or go without. The shoes seemed to symbolize all that had happened and Sarah knew Mama was right. She had to leave. She didn't have to like it.

"You are not helping the situation, Miss Long-Face," Mama said and followed Sarah halfway up the stairs. "Where are you off to now? We have to get an early start." And then in a softer tone, "You know, honey, we're going to find renters. And then we'll come back when the house payments are caught up. Honey?"

Oh, hush. Quit it. You don't need to be nice. We'll never come back and you don't care. You never wanted to live here anyway. Just because your daddy owned the coal mine and Daddy was a miner.

Mama hollered up the stairs as if she could read Sarah's mind. "You'll like it, you know. Hanlon is nice. You'll make friends, maybe a boyfriend, Sarah." Sarah clenched her fists and closed her eyes. Mama was always wanting her to have a boyfriend. It was sickening. Mama went on talking.

"This place here in Detroit? It's not so grand. It's exactly like any coal camp you've ever seen. These little tacky houses here on stamp-sized lawns? All alike. Just like a coal camp."

"Don't you believe it, Sarah." Uncle Marsh had come into the house from the driveway where he was packing the car. "Your Mama wouldn't know a coal camp if one rose up and smacked her in the face. Come on, Sis, tell me what you want where."

Sarah watched them go, Mama with her long auburn hair coiled in a lustrous knot on the back of her head, Uncle Marsh taller and slimmer with hair the color of pale sand curling around his ears and down into his collar. She said out loud after them, "I don't care what you say. I don't believe you. We'll never come back."

Now that they were out of the house, Sarah knew what she had to do. She moved quickly down the hall and into her room. Under the eaves in the bottom of a basket of old clothes, she found what she had hidden there the very first morning after Daddy. . . . She removed her sweater and blouse.

She pulled Daddy's white sleeveless undershirt on over

her own knitted underwear, first burying her face in the redolent cloth. She had hidden it, still sweaty and unwashed, with blood spattered across the front. She would wear it now. She needed it, like those suits of armor she'd seen at the art museum, needed it to hold in that hard lump of sadness and fury inside her body. With trembling fingers, before Uncle Marsh or Mama came looking for her, she buttoned her sweater again. Her heart pounded and yet she felt a strange relief. Nothing could hurt her now.

❧ 3 ❧

Buttoning her coat, Sarah went outside. A pale sun showed itself red above roofs of houses across the back alley. Mama and Uncle Marsh worked at the car.

"Where'd you get to?" Mama said. "Bring your Uncle Marsh that short piece of clothesline still hanging on the back door. There on the hook, will you? Please?"

"Lucey," Uncle Marsh said, "if we tie these suitcases on the running board, Sarah won't be able to get out the door. She'll have to sit back there with your potted fern and your sewing machine and I don't know what all for two whole days."

"It doesn't matter a bit in this world to Sarah, does it, honey?" Mama said and then didn't wait for Sarah's answer. "She can climb over things when she has to get out."

Sarah helped Uncle Marsh put boxes into the trunk of his car. As they worked she looked at him from beneath her eyelids. It was as though she couldn't stop, now that she had really looked at him. She wanted to memorize his face, his

14

high cheekbones and thin nose with the bony ridge. It wasn't the scar. The scar didn't matter anymore. What she gazed at, trying not to get caught, was her own face, she realized. Looking at Uncle Marsh was like looking into her own face.

She had always wanted to look like Mama and have red hair and brown eyes, wanted to be small and curved with full lips like Mama. She had never listened when Nancy told her she looked like an Indian princess in the movies, only she, Sarah, didn't know it yet. Now, she thought, I have this new face, this new person to look like. Having this new face was like taking powerful medicine. She felt it flow into her arms and down her legs.

Mrs. Drisdon came over from across the driveway, still wearing her nightclothes. She was bare-legged but wore her best Ruby shoes, twins of those that Sarah wore, tied in a neat bow below her nightgown and robe. Her gray hair was rolled up in little pink print rags all over her head. Sarah had never seen her in anything but all of her clothes. Even on the night Daddy died, Mrs. Drisdon watched it all from her front porch dressed to the nines, with her hair waved and metal taps on her heels. Daddy said the part he knew best about Mrs. Drisdon was her five fingers curled around her bathroom curtains, permanently folded back so she could watch what they did.

"Mrs. Raines, I've got some chicken here for your lunch on the road. It isn't much. It's the least I can. . . ." Sarah was certain there were tears in Mrs. Drisdon's pale eyes. "The mister and . . . we'll watch the house for you. If I can, I'll find renters. Right away. My brother might be interested."

"Thank you. Why, thank you, Mrs. Drisdon." Mama

spoke in that careful way she had learned in Detroit, not in the soft, slurry way Daddy and Uncle Marsh talked. Mama and Mrs. Drisdon always called each other by their married names, Sarah noticed, and wondered if she and her best friend, Nancy, would do that one day. If they ever saw each other again.

"Don't you worry about that," Mama added. "There are so many of these tacky little places around this part of the city, no one is going to want to rent from us. Why, people have to live anywhere they can these days. Didn't you hear the president talking on the radio last week? They live in tarpaper shacks. Railroad cars. For rent signs everywhere you look. No. You won't have to worry about it."

Sarah bit her tongue. *See, we'll never come back here to live. And I love it. Daddy loves it. He likes his swinging door leading into the kitchen. And his real bathroom with the toilet inside the house.* Sarah remembered how he laughed and told her he didn't have to tie himself to the side of the mountain to work in his garden anymore because it was as flat as a pancake in Detroit. But she knew he didn't think it was funny. He missed the mountains, she knew. But she didn't say anything about that. Instead, she pictured someone—a girl, maybe, her age—living in her house, going to school with Nancy, doing her homework on the kitchen table. The girl would play Mama's music, the operas Mama liked to play and sing and she would walk to school with Nancy each morning. Or play kick-the-can in the little park across the street. *Of course, now the neighborhood children won't want to play in the park ever again. Not since that night.* She hugged herself to see if the thin shirt Daddy had worn that night was still there, still protecting her, keeping feelings inside.

Uncle Marsh took off his hat and wiped his forehead with his shirt sleeve.

"Well, maybe we'll be lucky. We'll just hope you'll find somebody right soon." Uncle Marsh smiled down at Mrs. Drisdon that way he did, and Sarah thought Mrs. Drisdon was going to melt right there on the driveway, down into a little puddle of goodness.

"I'll do my best to." Mrs. Drisdon smiled up at Uncle Marsh.

"Yes, well, I reckon that's all we can hang on to. Hope. Times like these. Well. . . ." he turned to Mama. "You about ready to go? It's a two-day trip, Miz Drisdon," he said.

"The sooner the better, I always say. I'll just get on back in the house and let you folks go. Don't worry. I've got your key." Mrs. Drisdon backed down the driveway, her heels taps clicking. "I'll take care of things. A furnished house rents faster, don't you think?"

Mama followed Mrs. Drisdon a little way and then they hugged each other for the first and the last time that Sarah knew anything about.

"Oh, Marsh," Mama turned back. "I wonder . . . my roses. I hate to leave every single one of them. . . ."

Mama wrung her hands together the way she did when the man came to get their Ford car, repossessed it when they couldn't pay the payments anymore. "The Mrs. Herbert Hoover. It's so fragrant. Could we. . . ?"

"I'll show you, Mr. Stannard." Mrs. Drisdon recrossed the yard, her bathrobe flapping around her bare ankles. "I know just which one it is. Your sister has the most beautiful flowers and," she added, "the most beautiful voice. I used to listen. . . . You know what a good gardener she is?"

"Lead the way, Miz Drisdon," Uncle Marsh said. "Let's us dig Miz Herbert Hoover out of the ground in which she stands. We'll wrap her up in newspapers."

Mrs. Drisdon didn't smile. "Yes, and soak her in water. She'll travel better that way."

"Sarah, run and get me a spade, why don't you?" Uncle Marsh called.

As she went into the garage, Sarah thought that the rose would surely die, torn from its place that way.

Daddy's lawn mower sat in the corner. Brown dried grass still clung to the blades from the last mowing in the fall. Sarah squatted down to look. With beads of sweat popped out on his square forehead, Daddy had pushed that mower, cut that very same grass. It was, she thought, like God mowing people down. The grass was alive once and green. Now it was dead. She touched the grass, so dry and brittle that it fell apart in her hand. That was the way it was with people. First you were alive. Then you were dead. The only difference was, grass didn't go to heaven.

Daddy wouldn't go to heaven. How could he now, after what he'd done? Where would he go? Would he wander as he did when he didn't have a job to go to? She squinched her eyes and pushed the heaviness down inside where it wouldn't show. When she found the spade, she took it down from its place on the wall, laid it across both her arms stretched out in front of her. It was like someone's stiffened body. Mrs. Drisdon came into the garage just then, caught her holding the spade out before her like an offering, like a character in the movies at an exotic sacrificial altar. Mrs. Drisdon didn't seem to notice, just scuttled inside the garage, looking over her shoulder.

"Sarah." Her voice was quick and breathy. She tied and retied the belt to her robe, pulling it tighter across her big stomach each time she retied it.

"I've been wanting to speak to you, Sarah, ever since the funeral. I've been watching you. You are. . . ." She shook her head and the skin on her neck shook, too. She went on. "You have to be a good girl. Help your mother . . . your poor. . . ." Tears shone again in Mrs. Drisdon's eyes as she took Sarah's face in her cold hands. "If you misbehave, if you cry, your mother just might . . . die, too. You must promise you'll keep things to yourself. Keep quiet. Talk to God, but don't bother your mother." Mrs. Drisdon tied the robe one last time. "Why don't you just say it over to yourself so's you won't forget? 'I will not bother my mother now. I will be good all the time.'" *Or she might die*, Sara thought.

Sarah walked out of the garage, carrying the spade across her arms. She took long, stiff-legged steps. She was in the funeral procession in that Egyptian movie she had seen with Nancy. Mrs. Drisdon hurried over to Uncle Marsh just as the streetlights on the corner blinked off. The lights went off every morning at dawn, but this time it seemed to be a signal that Mrs. Drisdon was right. Sarah looked at Mama, looking for some sign that she might already be sick, maybe even at death's door, but Mama didn't seem any different. Sarah tried to picture what kind of door Death might be hiding behind.

At last, after Uncle Marsh had shaken hands with Mrs. Drisdon and Sarah had stood on one foot and then the other, they got into the car, Sarah in the backseat with the potted fern and the rose smelling of damp newspapers. Mrs. Drisdon bent down to look at her through the window. She

19

pointed her finger and mouthed some words to Sarah—those words that caused a knot in her stomach to harden. She wondered if she would be carsick, sick with the smell of gasoline and hard-boiled eggs they would peel and eat for their lunch along with the chicken Mrs. Drisdon brought. She moved the fern to another spot so she could look out the window. Mama rolled down her window, leaned out of the car, and waved and waved her handkerchief at Mrs. Drisdon. Sarah turned and sat on her knees to look out at her little house framed in the back window of the car. The house was just like all the others on the block and for three or four blocks all around. The only difference was that one was hers.

A pigeon fluttered across the path of the Hubmobile. Uncle Marsh took one turn around the little park and its dark clumps of shubbery at either end. She'd last seen her father there. Something tried to escape from her throat, a cry that she willed away. Turning to face front, she sat straight up, feet flat on the floor, hands folded deep in her lap. She stared at the back of Mama's head.

❧ 4 ❧

They drove all morning watching the sun rise and a thin biscuit moon disappear into a slit in the sky. Grocery stores and houses zipped past them as Sarah pretended it was the buildings and not she who traveled by so fast.

As they crossed the Ohio state line, Uncle Marsh hollered at Sarah in the backseat. "I beat you into Ohio by one-five-hundreth of a second!"

A pattern of new sights emerged: farms, earth, silos, barns, farmhouses, then towns with white-pillared courthouses around a square or an ornate church with its own graveyard in the center of town. As they passed one small churchyard cemetery, Sarah glimpsed reddish earth piled around a new grave. She shut her eyes. She heard the minister . . . *"dust thou art to dust returneth"* and saw her mother fall onto the ground, her breath coming out of her mouth like ghosts again. Mama must have read her mind.

"Lord, I wish we could have buried John Andrew in

Hanlon, at home. But, Marsh, money." She sighed. "Back home a burying was a wonderful thing."

"Back in Kentucky where your mama and daddy grew up"—Uncle Marsh kept his eyes on the road and half-turned to talk to Sarah over his shoulder—"everybody comes to a funeral. They come from all over the county. When we buried your grandmama and grandaddy after they died three weeks apart, everybody came. Had to come twice, as far as that goes. Brought food and flowers both times. Maybe your daddy would have had flowers, laurel that grows on the mountains."

Sarah had never seen laurel.

"They'd have dinner on the ground," Mama said, remembering, "served by the Lady's Aid Society?" Her voice rose in that questioning tone she used when she was pleased about something. "Everyone would sit around afterwards and tell stories about the dear departed."

If they could have had a real funeral in Hanlon, what stories would anybody tell about Daddy if they couldn't say anything about his terrible secret? She wasn't going to stand up in front of everyone and tell that he didn't have a job and lied to Mama. Or that he . . . the terrible word would not come. She could never tell the true story of John Andrew Raines, not even to Uncle Marsh.

She tried to imagine him, bring him forth in her mind's eye, tried to think of some good thing she could say.

He carried her, wrapped in blankets, into the living room and sat beside her on the couch. It was the middle of the night and Mama was there, rubbing her eyes and saying, "Are you crazy, John, waking us in the middle of the night?"

22

"How could I let y'all sleep and not see this amazing sight?" he said. And to Sarah: "It's an ice storm does this."

Across the street, on the other side of the park, where the streetcar tracks led into the city, a yellow streetcar, using its angled arm to help itself along, pushed its way through sleeves of thick ice encrusted on the overhead trolley lines. As ice fell away and the car moved slowly forward, glorious arcs of blue light lit up the snowy ground like a December Fourth of July.

"I wanted you to see, Sarah. Look! Just look at that, will you. I reckon you've never seen anything like that before or since!" he said. And she could smell the familiar sweet smell of whiskey on his breath. She watched as he seemed to take longer to move his arm or speak, as if he were underwater and trying to find his way out.

Blue light flashing illuminated the faces of people inside the street-car, lighted a path up the tracks, and glowed on Mama's and Daddy's faces close to her.

This is what she could tell, she thought. But before the words formed themselves in her mind, she stopped them. It is over and done with, she told herself. There'll be no chance to tell any stories about him. The last story is all there is to tell. She shuddered.

"One more thing, Sarah." Mama was still remembering and her voice sounded as if she were singing. "In Hanlon— well, everywhere in small towns, I reckon—when someone dies, they ring the passing bell. One long ring for every year the person lived on this earth? When the bell your grand-mama gave to the church tolls out across the hills, oh! . . ."

Mama waved her arm as if there were no words powerful enough to tell how grand it was. There was no bell when Daddy was buried. No laurel branches. Only damp, cold

23

wind and Mama falling onto the bare earth heaped up around the grave.

They drove deeper into spring as they traveled south. Soon Sarah saw yellow forsythia and apple trees blooming pink and white in orchards. In some places, black bottom land was already turned over and green shoots appeared in low, damp corners of squared-off fields.

Sarah forgot for a while that she was practically being kidnapped, taken away from her real home and her best friend. She listened to Mama and Uncle Marsh talk about Hanlon and who was still there and who wasn't.

"Yep," Uncle Marsh told Mama, "the Block twins are still livin' next door. Both deaf as doornails now. But they're lookin' forward to having you back!"

"What about Aunt Sude, poor old Aunt Sude?" Mama said.

Sarah remembered that Aunt Sude used to work for Grandmama Stannard when Mama and Uncle Marsh were children, and now Aunt Sude was way up in her nineties. Now Keziah, Aunt Sude's daughter, worked for Uncle Marsh. Sarah couldn't imagine what it would be like to have someone to cook and clean up for you the way Nancy Pettibone's mother had.

"Aunt Sude's a little *non compos mentis* sometimes," Uncle Marsh said. "But on her good days when she's not so confused, she can tell you something about everybody in town. Sometimes it is something folks would just as soon not be mentioned right out before God and everybody! Aunt Sude has gotten right mean in her old age, I'm afraid. Lord, I try to stay away from her. Keziah brings her up to the house and she irons some. But it is untellin' what she will say right out of the blue."

"Poor thing, she always did have a sharp tongue, but she wasn't downright mean," Mama said. "I do remember Keziah had a hard time, even back when I was a girl, keeping Aunt Sude from just blurting out all her resentments about white folks. . . ."

"Well, can you blame her?" Uncle Marsh said.

There was a long, silent time and then Mama said, "What about the depression? Is it as awful in Kentucky as it is in Detroit?"

"I manage, Lucey. I'm lucky. I still own the newspaper, you know. People will always want their newspaper, I reckon. That little truck mine I bought from Daddy? Well, it keeps me in cigarette money. It's not worth much when no one can buy coal."

Uncle Marsh seemed to slow the car down automatically when he talked about hard times. "Hard times, you might say, don't make no never mind to poor, old folks like Aunt Sude. It's all the same to them."

"I read about these children in Tennessee?" Sarah joined in the talk without thinking, without remembering that she could never join in or let them see anything but how sad she was. "These children?" she said again. "Well, they were so hungry they gnawed on their arms to have something to eat. In Tennessee."

"Sarah! What a thing to say. People? Babies? Eat themselves? You are plumb crazy," Mama said without looking back at Sarah, slumped now on the backseat.

There it was again, Mama saying she was crazy. Usually

she said, "Crazy like all the rest of the Raineses." Sarah wished she could think of something to do that was really crazy. She stared out the window and thought about the babies who had to eat their own arms. Would they leave little teeth marks in their flesh or would they have to suck out the juices to get the good of it? She bit into her own arm. It tasted salty.

"Heckfire," she said because Mama didn't want her to say "heckfire." What she really wanted to say was "hellfire and damnation," the way Nancy Pettibone did. Nancy got it from Thelma. Sarah wondered if Keziah would be anything like Thelma, Nancy's maid, who slept on Nancy's four-poster bed when Mrs. Pettibone was away and who let the girls curse.

"Heckfire," she said it again, louder this time. "From what I hear, people in Kentucky and Tennessee are worse off than we are in Detroit. No jobs there either. I don't imagine we'll stay very long."

Telephone poles along the straight road slipped by one by one as Sarah was lulled by the sound of the tires against the smooth road. Uncle Marsh leaned against the car door, pushed his hat back off his forehead, and the car sped along. Sarah slept.

The supper table lay on its back, its legs straight up in the air like an old dog playing dead. Mama's china cabinet was toppled onto its side. Out from its shelves Grandmama's hand-painted dishes spilled across the patterned rug like garbage scattered by crows in the alley. The window was broken and a few shards of glass left in the frame caught at thin curtains and held them billowing, ghost sails in the night wind.

26

A blurred white shape hurried across their patch of lawn. A quick, blue light flashed, one sudden burst of blue light with a hot red center that came before the sound. It was the backfiring of a car, she told herself. But when Mama's scream came, Sarah knew what the sound and the burst of light were.

"Aaagh! Aaagh! Aaagh!"

Mama shrieked high and thin as if her mouth was wide open. A man shouted, doors slammed in the night, footsteps echoed between the houses as neighbors awakened and ran into the park where moaning and crying out loud were the only sounds.

"I want my daddy!" She yelled it into the darkness of her room. Like vomit, the words came out of her mouth before she could stop them. Once they were out, she would not stop them.

"I want my daddy!"

She wanted to run, to find him, to help him somehow. She longed to put her cheek on his head, feel the squareness of his skull beneath flat, curled hair against her face, but she could not move. Why was she such a coward, afraid, afraid of what she might find? Her mouth was dry as chalk dust. Still, she could not move. Mama screamed again.

"Mama, where are you?"

She was outside then, somehow. A sudden slap of cold air bit her face and bare legs. Shadowy figures in the park, moving as if through waves of heat from a house afire, hesitated, poised above something on the ground momentarily, then bent, lifted, touched something on the ground. Flashlights shuddered across her face.

"Daddy!"

Down across her shoulders and chest came rough arms with hair on them as car lights shone like beacons on her father, faceless, lying on red ground.

❧ 5 ❧

Sarah's face shook from remembering so hard. She couldn't
move. Her mother's voice streamed back to her as if through
a tunnel. Mama said, "Promise me . . . promise." Mama said
it again. "Marsh, promise me you will not tell a soul about
John Andrew. I will not have everyone in town talking
shame behind my back. Feeling sorry. Judging. It was bad
enough in Detroit. People looking the other way. . . ."

"Aw, 'shaw, Lucey. You're imagining."

"Not a soul. Not Keziah. And especially not Aunt Sude.
Think with her mean tongue what she'd—"

"I'm not going to say anything to anybody, if that's what
you want."

"I do."

"You'll never keep it from old Aunt Sude. She knows everything."

It was raining hard now. Water swam across the car windows, swam against the river of glass like little tadpoles. It

was hot: steamy quiet filled the car. Only the windshield wiper could be heard: *thunka, thunka, thunk.* Sarah never thought Mama would tell their secret, so secret they had never spoken it aloud even to each other. Even back home in their little house when they'd catch each other staring out the front window into the park, they never spoke of it. And now Mama had told Uncle Marsh that Daddy was crazy and wouldn't go to heaven.

"It doesn't bother me. You know that, don't you? I don't think any less of John Andrew," Uncle Marsh said.

"You don't." Mama put the accent on "you."

"No. I'm only sorry for—"

"Maybe you don't, but I do."

"Lucey, why?"

"I can't help myself. It was wrong. Wrong." Mama's voice rose.

"Hush now, Lucey, you don't want to waken Sarah."

There was a pause. Sarah had to take one small shallow breath. Mama spit out the next words and didn't seem to mind if she woke Sarah or not.

"He's a sinner. He'll not get to heaven."

The heaviness in Sarah's chest swelled like a balloon filled with water. She felt that drowning might be like this. She wanted to yell at Mama, to hurt her somehow. She put her hands over her mouth, pressed her face deeper into the gray car seat. She could not breathe again. She made herself remember what Mrs. Drisdon told her . . . "your mother will die too, if you don't keep quiet." *And then what would become of you?*

Uncle Marsh said, "Oh, Lucey, honey, you reckon he's

going to be laid where the nettles grow, where all the unbaptized babies, drunks, and others of the 'conjecturally damned' are laid?"

"Ahhh, don't get bookish with me, you know as well as I do. . . ."

"That can't be much comfort to you." Sarah heard him take a long drink of Co'Cola, as he put it, heard the liquid gurgle through the neck of the green bottle.

"Mercy!" Mama's voice swam in the wind over the seat back. "Mercy!" She cried out again. "My Lord, why are you punishing me this way? What did I do? Marsh, I can't go on. Is it ever going to end?" Mama sobbed. "I miss him. Even with all the trouble. The lies. Him drinking. What will I do without him?"

Why did Mama think Uncle Marsh knew what to do? Did Mama feel about him the way she, Sarah, was beginning to? Sarah turned onto her back, stared at the glass-covered ceiling light. The blank eye seemed to ask her where her father would go if not to heaven. Would Daddy wander around forever somewhere in between heaven and hell and never find a resting place? Or would he simply burn in everlasting hellfire the way Mrs. Drisdon said he would at the funeral? And, if he burned, Sarah asked the Eye, how could she go on in her life knowing that? Was this what the preacher meant when he said, "visiting the sins of the fathers upon the children unto the third generation?"

"He was crazy." Mama said it low and slow. "Crazier than Wanda." She seemed to be thinking now about Daddy's sister. Sarah closed her eyes again. *Don't cause trouble, don't.*

"Does that woman still live alone and wander up and

30

down the hills all times of the day and night, the way she used to?"

"She might be a little queer, Lucey. But she's about as crazy as you and me."

"See? She *is* crazy, then. Like all the rest of us," Mama said and you could almost hear her begin to smile at her own joke. "What did I tell you?"

They drove along then with just the swishing sound of tires against the streaming road and the windshield wipers slapping back and forth. Sarah tried her best to forget that Mama had told their secret. Though she felt betrayed, she forced herself to remember only Mrs. Drisdon's words. She felt a headache begin. She reached inside her blouse to touch Daddy's undershirt, but the hurt would not go away.

Uncle Marsh wiped steam off the front window with his forearm and he said, "Oh, Lucey, listen. How do we know what God forgives and doesn't forgive? He knows us. But we can't know Him. What kind of God is it whom I know? We can't know what God thinks about John Andrew."

"He tells us, all right," Mama said. "In the Bible. In His Commandments. In the earth. Everywhere."

Sarah smelled the acrid smell of a match being lit. Cigarette smoke drifted back.

"That's true." Uncle Marsh blew out a long breath. "And He tells us not to judge. We have to forgive because we need forgiveness so desperately ourselves."

"When you can tell me how to do that . . . I'll . . . I can't forgive or forget. Not yet."

Uncle Marsh asked Mama if she recalled the time their

papa and some of his cronies cornered a bobcat there by the Courthouse downtown. "She'd come down off the mountain somehow and brought her kits with her?"

Mama said she remembered. "Hungry, I reckon. That was the year it was so dry everything like to burned up."

"Well, John Andrew couldn't stand it. He was just a kid, remember? He had a conniption fit, right downtown in front of everybody. Papa shot . . . killed the mother. But John Andrew put those kittens in a box and wouldn't let Papa drown them. I never did know what he did with them."

"Reckon he took them up to Wanda's house, don't you, for her to do something with? Papa never forgave him for it, whatever he did with them. Never forgave him that first humiliation no more than he did the second: marrying me."

"Lucey, no matter what you think now, John Andrew was a good man."

"I know it. I know," Mama began. "So why? Why?" The last why came out so long and mournful that Sarah had to hold her breath again. She felt that she would rise up and go right through the top of the car if she heard any more or thought any more about any of it. She curled into the smallest ball she could and imagined that someone was squeezing all her innards with one big, hot hand. When she could let herself, she looked at the Mrs. Herbert Hoover rose; the faint green and little pink nipples on the stem seemed to fade before her eyes.

At dusk the rain stopped. They drove along the slanting escarpment above the Ohio River through towns clinging to the riverbank. Beyond them lay rounded shapes of purple and blue, becoming green mountains. After they floated across the tan waters of the Ohio on a paddle-wheel ferry, they found a tourist court on the Kentucky side and rented white painted cabins with screening tacked across wide windows facing fresh tarred road. Sarah took off her clothes in a corner of the little room while Mama cleaned out the car. She could not let Mama see the undershirt she wore. When Mama finished undressing, she stood at the opened door as the light from a metal-shaded lamp shone into the room from outside.

Sarah could see only Mama's profile with its one almond eye. It looked to Sarah like those on the Greek—or was it Roman?—heads at the Detroit Art Institute. She couldn't remember, and now, she supposed, she would never see the beautiful heads there again. Strands of Mama's hair had escaped the heavy knot on the back of her neck. She removed strings of it from her eyes and mouth. Mama looked hot.

"I thought you wanted your hair cut off before. . . ?" Sarah said. "Isn't it awfully hot and sweaty?"

"Oh, law', honey," Mama was talking Kentucky again. "I just couldn't do it. Not now. Your daddy . . ." She swallowed hard. "Your daddy said my hair was my crowning glory. He didn't want for me to cut it. I reckon I'll just have to leave it this way . . . now."

Mama reached back, elbows angled up, head tipped forward, eyes closed. She found the hidden pins and she unpinned the heavy knot of hair by heart.

Before she fell asleep in the bed she shared with Mama, curled together like memories, Sarah heard Uncle Marsh

33

cough in the next cabin, smelled his cigarette as the smoke floated into their window. With a buzzing noise, three large white moths threw themselves against the light bulb outside her door. Somewhere in the distance a dove's mournful cooing sounded like rain or death.

It was true, true what Nancy had said about doves and death, that their cooing meant someone had died. Of course it was true. Wasn't she living proof of it?

6

"Are we here?"

Sarah leaned over the front seat and folded her arms across the bristly seat back. It was the end of the second day on the road.

"Yessir! We've landed all in one piece. Put a quarter in your thank box, just to say thanks for a safe trip, honey."

Uncle Marsh opened his window and pounded on the side of the car with one hand. Cold air blew in on Sarah, bringing strong, strange smells of smoke and flowers. Uncle Marsh drove faster now.

"Mind now, Marshall Newton Stannard," Mama said. "We've come all this way. Let's not get in a wreck now." But she smiled when she said it.

They had driven all day along a road that wound itself around the shoulders of mountains and sometimes crossed rocky creek beds, "crooked as a dog's hind leg," Uncle Marsh said. They snaked back and forth on hairpin turns to meet themselves coming and going. Like a fresh gash on the earth, the road ran along the side of the mountain—a raw, rocky face on one side and a deep green valley on the other. Trees were so dense in the valleys that Sarah couldn't see through to the ground below. She stared down, wondering if people had to walk across the tops of trees to get where they wanted to go.

It had grown dark. Mama fell asleep finally and Sarah sat up to watch the road and the red tip of Uncle Marsh's cigarette as they came into small coal camps settled into gaps between the mountains. Their headlights shone into the dusk, pointing their way. Uncle Marsh was quiet and she felt that closeness again, being in the dark car with the mountains like solid walls surrounding them.

And now here they were, in Hanlon, driving up Laurel Street. Sarah knew about Laurel Street. This was where Mama and Uncle Marsh grew up, the street built by King Coal, as Mama put it. White houses with pointed gables and low, wide porches or stone mansions lined the cobblestoned street while Laurel Hill loomed in the background.

Before they left Detroit, Uncle Marsh drew a map for Sarah with colored pencils, pencils Daddy had used to sketch Mama's picture sometimes as they sat at the kitchen table after supper. On Uncle Marsh's map, red was for Grandaddy's white house where they would live now; blue for the church where Mama used to sing solos and play the piano, black for the school Sarah would attend in the fall (if they stayed that long), the same one Mama and Uncle Marsh went to. Yellow pencil was for the Dixie-Grande, where Sarah could see movies, and for Uncle Marsh's newspaper office downtown near the Courthouse. Green was for her cousin Beth Ann's house up on Laurel Hill, looking down on all the

rest of us, Uncle Marsh said, and for Aunt Wanda Raines'
house farther out of town at the top of some remote hollow
place between mountains. When Mama protested Aunt
Wanda's inclusion on the map, Uncle Marsh said, "Why,
certainly Sarah will go to visit her aunt. She's the last living
relative she's got on the Raines side of the family."

"All right," Mama said. "Then she'll have to meet her
cousin Beth Ann, too. She's seventeen and already a real
lady. You told me so yourself."

The map, however carefully Uncle Marsh fashioned it, did
not prepare Sarah for the way things really looked. No one
told her how the mountains wrapped around you until you
couldn't see a way out of them nor about the rich, smoky
smell of the night air. She had not expected to see stone
walkways that disappeared like questions around corners of
walls, nor ivy-covered houses and garages made of stone and
cut into the face of the hill. It was nothing like her flat,
square yard at home.

"Sarah, look there on the corner. There's the Methodist
Church." The church was a columned building with one oval
window made of colored glass in a latticed bell tower. "Well,
well, the bell is still there. Your grandmama donated that,
honey." Mama's voice seemed to sing like the very bell she
pointed out to Sarah.

Crickets and night birds and other little rustling things
sang in the dark, the blue dark. Sarah was cold. Her eyes
watered and she bounced up and down on the backseat,
being careful not to knock over the potted fern or the rose.
She bounced as much to warm herself as to ease the tense-
ness in her body, to keep the butterflies in her stomach from
flying out of her mouth. "Hey!" Uncle Marsh peered out

37

through the bug-splattered, dusty windshield. "Look, at that, will you? All those people up on our front porch? This time of night?"

He leaned forward, put both hands on the wheel and stepped on the gas.

"I declare, Marsh, looks like the whole county's payin' you a call," Mama said.

Old Model T's, new light-colored roadsters, a black dust-covered touring car or two, all were parked every which way on both sides of the street. People milled around the yard. Women in pale dresses stood on the front walk. Men in shirt sleeves and suspenders smoked and laughed near the gate. Chasing each other, children darted like butterflies into and out of the yard.

"Well, I declare!"

"What on earth?"

Mama and Uncle Marsh kept repeating themselves.

"Hey, y'all, what's goin' on?" Uncle Marsh stopped the car right in the middle of the street and swung out of the door. Sarah was transfixed. She was certain that all these people, the children, the men and women whom she did not know, were there to welcome her. She couldn't believe they would come, but of course she did believe. She felt confirmed, close to tears of relief after all the days of worry and sadness, after the fears about coming to a new place. To come here and find this! How could she have doubted it? She yearned over the figures in the yard. They seemed to her now to be friends, people she'd known all her life.

7

Sarah struggled out of the car where she had ridden for two long days packed in with all their earthly belongings. She climbed over the sewing machine, the music books Mama had wanted to throw away but Uncle Marsh had said, "No, bring them; you'll sing again," the potted fern, which hadn't seemed to mind the trip, and the Mrs. Herbert Hoover rose, which did. Sarah's hair sprang up all over her head. Her stockings turned every which way and no one seemed to notice, least of all Mama, who normally would have licked the palm of her hand to slick Sarah's hair and have signaled her to straighten her stockings or pull up her slip.

Uncle Marsh had Mama by the hand and they ran into the yard ahead of Sarah. Sarah wasn't willing to break the spell of welcome by stepping into the circle of yellow light and merriment. Not yet.

"Jimmy? That you? Why, Miz Watkins, what're you doin' here? Thought you'd be up listenin' to Amos and Andy on the radio tonight."

Uncle Marsh's voice floated above the others. He spoke, Sarah noticed, with his mountain accent just as though he'd never been to Princeton or Paris, France.

"Marshall, old son, we been waitin' for ye. Y'all got here just in time, I reckon. Tomorrow it'll be about gone," someone said.

"Say what?" Uncle Marsh said. "What'll be gone?"

Did he think that everyone was here to meet him the way Sarah did? Of course, he felt it, too. Sarah clasped her hands together.

"The flower, old son, the flower. Your mama planted it years ago? I reckon while you were over fightin' in the war . . ."

"Only blooms once ever' hundred years, so they say."

". . . Law', Marshall, you almost didn't get here in time."

"Marsh? He's old Mr. Ben-Puttin'-It-Off. I declare, that boy'll be late to his own wedding."

"Marsh Stannard? Married? Not him!"

Everybody laughed and pounded Uncle Marsh on the back and kissed Mama and told her they were sorry to hear about John Andrew Raines. "That makes ever' one of those Raines boys dead and gone," they said and shook their heads and held Mama's hands in theirs, asking her if she was going to sing solos up at church again the way she used to do.

Uncle Marsh kissed a tall woman, or was she just a girl? Sarah couldn't tell, because she had short yellow hair like Nancy Pettibone, but she wore a woman's silky dress. The other women, Mama included, wore cottony prints wrapped around and tied to the side, had long hair coiled in a knot. The girl-woman's dress fluttered around her long legs like little flags and Sarah didn't like her one bit hanging on to

Uncle Marsh that way. Sarah felt sickness rise in her throat, and she knew it wasn't from riding in the car all day.

It turned out, after all the greetings and the sympathies extended to Mama about John Andrew's death, that everyone had come to see the century plant which had never bloomed before—the *Agave virginica*, the girl-woman called it. Grandmama had planted it years ago. Why it chose tonight of all nights to bloom was something Sarah didn't understand, but there it was like a queen in its large ceramic pot.

"Hey! Here's Lucey's girl. Bless her heart."

"Come on, little missy. Come on over here in the good light. Let us get a better look at you, why don't you, honey?"

"Why, where's your pretty red hair like your mama's, child?"

"I declare, Marshall, she takes after you."

"She's so tall."

Sarah turned from speaker to speaker, trying to sort out all their words. She was tired. The sense of joy and welcome ran out of her like water when she saw it was the flower they'd come to see and not her. Not Mama either. But the thing about it was, Mama didn't seem to mind. She was too busy accepting condolences and kissing everyone. A tall woman with frizzy white hair nodded at Sarah. Sarah knew the milk-chocolate woman was Keziah Jordan, who had taken care of Mama and Uncle Marsh for all those years, so she nodded back. Keziah stood just inside the screen door and chewed on a stick. She didn't speak—not, that is, until Mama came running up on to the porch.

"Keziah! This is my Sarah." Keziah nodded again and

looked at Sarah as if she'd been looking at her every day since the day she was born.

And then Keziah and Mama hugged again and again with tears in their eyes.

"Everything looks . . . smaller, Keziah. Even you," Mama said.

And they stood there, not saying a word to Sarah, when an old, straight-haired woman swinging her cane back and forth like a whip, came to the front door and asked to use the bathroom. She disappeared into the house.

"Lord, Keziah, Aunt Min Stannard will likely rise up out of her coffin and tell everybody she's got to find the bathroom! Nothing's changed," Mama said.

"Hunh! You still the same dreamer you always was. Everything's changed, girl. And its goin' to keep on that way." Keziah took hold of both Mama's shoulders and looked right square at her. "I'm mighty glad you're home," she said.

Then someone else said, "Looka here, little missy, that's your grandmother's flower. Your Grandmother Stannard? Ain't it a sight in this world?"

Sarah forced herself to look at the waxy, yellow-green flower atop a tall stalk. She tried to think about her grandmother putting it into the blue pot, watering it for those years, expecting it to bloom. But she had no clear picture of Grandmama Stannard and she couldn't imagine the cluster of blossoms coming so long after Grandmama died. Its thick fragrance filled her nostrils. Several people stood around the wicker stand like worshippers at the feet of some exotic foreign idol in Nancy's favorite Saturday serials at the movies back home in Detroit. The worshippers came onto the porch one by one and Sarah thought for a moment somebody might kneel down, but nobody did. Instead, drawn by the fragrance, they leaned forward to gaze up at the funnel-shaped flowers, their hands clasped behind their backs. There was noise and movement on the street or in the yard. Here on the porch people whispered.

"Is it true? It dies after it blooms?"

"No. No, that's not true at all."

With a sense of relief, Sarah turned to see who spoke in such a loud, matter-of-fact way and didn't act as if she were in church. It was the girl-woman with her arm in Marsh's arm. Uncle Marsh ducked his head and listened carefully to what she was going to say next in her dry, husky voice. He fingered the thickest part of his scar, which Sarah had never seen him do before.

"There are many legends about it . . . that it dies, that it blooms only once in one hundred years, that it blooms only one night," the girl-woman said as if she were addressing a class. "None of these are true."

"You tell 'em, schoolteacher," someone out in the yard said. The crowd broke up with little disappointed laughs. Everything seemed changed by the girl-woman.

"Well, Miss Amanda Bennet, hit's a sight prettier than ever' bit of laurel and dogwood so common out there on the hillsides."

The person who said this said it softly, as if she did not want it to be heard. Sarah heard. It was Keziah from inside the screen door in the shadows.

Sarah didn't know what to do now. Mama was encircled by old friends and relatives. Uncle Marsh fingered his scar and talked to Miss Amanda Bennet. Everyone else laughed and talked, seemed to belong together. The smell of the flower reminded her of the time she spilled some of Mama's "Evening in Paris" perfume. The odor clung to her hands for days, and of course Mama discovered her crime.

Now she stared at the flower so hard tears came to her eyes. She hung her head and her shoulders curved in toward each other. She wanted to sink down, down into the earth, and never be heard from again.

"Sarah?" She heard her mother's voice, half concerned, half embarrassed. "You all right? Don't you want to stand up nice and straight, honey?"

Sarah had not cried since she saw Mr. Drisdon and the others carry her father into the house with the burlap bag over his ruined head. She didn't cry when Mrs. Drisdon said he would burn in hell and took his shirt, saying that it was too good to throw away. All it needed was a good washing, she whispered. Sarah hadn't even cried when Mama told their secret to Uncle Marsh.

Now, of all terrible times, the tears started and slid down her cheeks. She tried to stop them by holding her breath, which only made her snort the way a child might. She felt as if she were dying and Daddy's undershirt, her armor, wasn't helping.

"She's tired. Can't they see that? Poor child's plumb wore out." *That voice again.* "Mr. Marshall!" it said louder.

Uncle Marsh picked her up then as Keziah led the way into the dark, cool house. Uncle Marsh told her things were going to get better.

"Mind now, what I say, things will be all right. Soon, soon." He crooned, "Now then, honey, now then, honey," over and over. Keziah opened doors and padded silently in carpet slippers down the long, long hall in front of Uncle

Marsh until they came into a small bedroom with a ceiling so low that he had to bend a little to enter the door. It smelled of spice and talcum powders and dried flowers, not the kind you pick fresh from the garden. Its walls were covered with flowered paper and high windows opened to the night air. Spread with a crocheted coverlet with tassled fringe hanging down in points on either side, a large iron bedstead painted white sat under the windows. There was a patchwork quilt with patterns of bell-like flowers beneath the coverlet. Keziah turned down the bedclothes and Sarah felt the fragrance of Fels-Naptha soap wash over her. When Uncle Marsh put her down, it seemed she would fall forever into feathered air with warmth and softness enfolding her. When she came at last to the depths of the feather bed, she slept.

❧ 8 ❧

No familiar streetlights shone into this room. No streetcar clanged along the tracks across Oakland Boulevard. No, she told herself, this is Grandmama Stannard's bed. I am here in Hanlon, not at home in Detroit.

Faint light reached her through high windows and the room bloomed palely in semidark. Sarah peered across the room to a graceful highboy on one wall. Next to it an open closet emerged in the dimness. Hanging inside she saw her two-piece dress with the peplum she'd worn in the car. If someone had undressed her and hung her dress there, where was Daddy's undershirt? She needed her armor. *Mama will surely take it away if she sees it.* How could she ever begin to tell Mama about it? It was too much like a diary you'd write in. No, like a prayer. Sarah felt the soft fabric of her night-gown and inside, bare and damp from the feather bed, only her own skin. The undershirt was gone. She threw back the bedclothes. She had to get out of the suffocating feather bed, which suddenly smelled old and full of mold. She misjudged the distance from the iron bedstead to the floor. It was farther from the floor than her own bed at home and she fell onto her hands and knees. She stayed that way, just looking down at the braided rug, not wanting to wake anyone with a cry. She didn't even know where Mama was; asleep somewhere in this strange, big house.

She felt her way into the closet where she fumbled around in musty dimness that smelled of moth and mouse and lavender. She found only her own underclothes, her navy blue old-lady shoes with stockings rolled neatly inside. She must find a light. Moving slowly around the room, touching a chair, a trunk, a soft footstool, she felt shapes, nothing else. She stumbled into a mirror on a stand reflecting a pumpkin face, her own, back at her. The mirror flipped forward, knocking a small chair onto its side with a muffled sound. *Where is the light?* Finally, on a small wicker table beneath the window, a table filled with books, she found a lamp and pulled the little chain to light it. Sarah rocked back and forth on the rug. How would she manage without Daddy's smell to have close? She remembered Mrs. Drisdon's words, pictured her mother lying on her back upstairs somewhere with one arm flung out across the empty pillow next to her and the other lying across her eyes, as if she didn't want to see anything anymore.

Then she noticed it. A drawer in the top section of the highboy was open, almost as if someone had left it that way on purpose. Everything else, she thought, is as if no one had ever come in until tonight.

Inside the drawer, hidden beneath a pile of lace-edged handkerchiefs, was the shirt. Unwashed. She buried her face in it again and breathed in and then slipped it on. Mama, she thought, wouldn't have done this. She was too busy talking and saying, "Yes, it was very unexpected for all of us. Heart, you know."

Uncle Marsh? No. She was too old for that. It was Keziah who had helped her and that made two times in one night. Yes, it was Keziah, she was certain.

She wrapped her arms around herself, feeling the only part of her father that was not taken away from her in a box. She felt herself grow stronger. It was time to see the rest of the house. She opened the bedroom door. Outside was a narrow hall, the same hall down whose length Uncle Marsh had carried her. Light gleamed stronger now to the left, to the back of the house. She walked toward the light into a large kitchen. On the sink board she found a glass. She ran water into it and drank deeply in thirsty gulps. Over the rim of the glass, she saw that the whole room and everything in it seemed big, bigger than anything in their little house back home. Uncle Marsh had a new Frigidaire refrigerator just like Nancy Pettibone's with round coils like a hat on top. Next to it was a circular oaken table with high-backed chairs around it. The room smelled of coal oil and old linoleum and cooking.

At one side of the kitchen there was a swinging door with a little window in it so you could see if someone was coming through the other way. Now Sarah knew why Daddy liked his swinging door so much. She pushed through the door into a little room lined with shelves to the ceiling. On some of the lower shelves, china dishes waited next to silver teapots and trays. She fingered the thin, fluted edge of one fragile cup and thought about Daddy holding it, his coal-blackened knuckles wrapped around the curved handle.

She stood there in the dark remembering how Daddy would throw open the swinging door and blunder into Mama's steamy kitchen, taking up all the room. He'd kiss Mama and Sarah, too. He'd gather them up in his blue-shirted arms, hunch over them, and Sarah knew then that the sour breath and the sweet songs and the kissing were somehow connected. He never kissed them otherwise and certainly did not talk so much. Sarah loved him even though he had the evil drink inside him. She loved him, but she was afraid. She never knew what to believe, love or fear.

"Now, Sarah," he'd say, "you don't know it, but my great-grandpap came from Virginny back in the seventeen-hundreds. Owned a whole valley in them days. A land ownin' educated man he was, too. Bet ye didn't know that, now, did ye?"

"Nossir." But she did.

And then, "Of course, now there's your mama. Now she has a real education. She can sing, opera, even." He'd giggle. "Miss Monrie's FEE-male Academy."

His voice would keen off into laughter about fee-males at school until Mama would march herself into the bathroom and lock the door against him and then he'd lean—no, it was more that, he would *sag*—into the door, jiggle the knob and beg Mama through the closed door to come on out. Finally, Mama would edge herself out of the bathroom, feeling the knot of hair on her neck and smelling of "Evening in Paris" and Sarah would be sent off to the store for a pint of Miller's ice cream.

Now, she went outside onto the porch. Framed by the light-ening sky, the mountains rose above the house. Sarah felt closed in but not oppressed. Instead, the mountains made a nest for her the same as her cavelike room under the eaves at home. The waning moon flickered through trees and slivered light onto dew-covered grass. In its blue pot the century plant exhaled its sick, sweet odor. The blossoms on the tall stalk were hidden in darkness now. Sarah hugged herself inside her nightgown, her arms cold against Daddy's undershirt.

And then, without thinking what she was going to do, she broke the cluster of blossoms from the woody stem. Carrying the flower, she ran into the front yard under the young oak trees. Caught by a breath of air as she threw it, the blossoms floated there for a moment. Then, as she watched, it fell into the branches of the oak.

9

"Looks like a star up there, doesn't it?"

How long had Uncle Marsh been standing there in the shadows? Of course, he'd seen her take the flower, everybody's wonderful flower. He'd seen her throw it as far as she could. Now he would tell Mama. She rubbed the sticky liquid on the side of her nightgown.

Uncle Marsh stepped onto the front walk, carrying his suit coat over his shoulder. Sarah wondered why he was still dressed as he was last night. Hadn't he been to bed at all? His sandy hair was tousled over his forehead in a way she'd never seen before. He looked like her favorite movie stars, Randolph Scott and Clark Gable, rolled into one. Even if he told Mama, which he was sure to do, Mama wouldn't be apt to do anything about it. Now that she was back in Hanlon where she'd wanted to be all the fifteen years she lived with Daddy in Detroit, Sarah was sure she would pay even less attention to her than before. There was something so quiet about Mama now, as if she was waiting for something, as if she was the only person who knew a terrible secret. Not Daddy's secret, but another one.

"Maybe it's a star." Uncle Marsh continued to walk toward her. Now half his face could be seen in the light from the moon, the pure, clean half, without the scarring.

"Maybe," he said, "it will bring good fortune to all those who stand beneath this tree."

"No," she said, "I don't think so. There's no such a-thing."

He put his hand on her shoulder and she wanted to bury her face in his side and have him hold her. His hand felt full and warm through the thin material of her gown. But she drew away.

"Things die, Sarah," he said. He said it simply, as if they'd been talking about it all along.

"I guess I know that." Unblinking, she looked at him. What would he say next?

"People die. Flowers die. You can ruin one blossom by throwing it away. You could say that's what your daddy did. Threw away his life. But he didn't kill the plant. And neither did you." He led her back to the ceramic planter on its stand. "If you look, you'll see another little plant forming. Down here at the base. It's coming. People are like that, you know. Part of us always lives on."

He put both arms around her and now she was able to return the embrace. His body was warm and smelled like air itself. He touched her hair.

"You miss him, I reckon. You'll get over your grievin' . . . he's not lost forever. You'll find more to love."

Sarah felt a knot untie somewhere inside her and slither away. Still, there were so many questions.

"But he's not . . . not going to heaven. I know," she said. "He's burning in hell. Mama said. Mrs. Drisdon did, too. And the preacher."

"That's what you think, then?"

"No. Yes. It's a commandment, isn't it? Not to kill? Doesn't that mean yourself, too?"

"You know what I think? I think John Andrew was already in hell, right here on earth. First his brothers were killed in the war and he couldn't go to avenge them. Somehow, he blamed himself. Then he lost his job. All that pretending he did so he wouldn't look bad in your mother's eyes. No money comin' in. Well. . . ." He wrapped his jacket around Sarah's shoulders. "Maybe we'll never know what or why," he said.

They sat on the front steps. Sarah thought how Daddy couldn't let himself be anything less than perfect, even in Mama's eyes. Maybe *especially* in front of Mama. No grown-up had ever talked to her like this. This was the way it was with Nancy. Now she needed to know what Uncle Marsh believed about other things.

"Don't you believe in hellfire and damnation?"

"No," he said. "No, I don't. Nor golden streets like they sing in the hymn. Sarah honey, your daddy was a good man. He wanted to be right. Can you find it in your heart to forgive him? When you can do that, you'll see. It'll be better for you, then."

Sarah didn't think she could ever forgive Daddy. How could Uncle Marsh ask it? How could she when Daddy chose to leave her and Mama? How did he think they would pay the rent? Or buy coal and food? Had he known that Uncle Marsh would rescue them? Why couldn't Daddy be rescued, too?

Uncle Marsh said, "It's too early to get up. Go on back to bed now." He went upstairs and she found her way back to the little room and the high-legged bed. She slept again and, in that hour before full daylight, for the first time in a long time, she did not dream of a lake of fire and saving someone from the burning circle.

Sarah thought that everybody in town wondered about it, but Mama never did say a word about the century plant or the missing cluster of blossoms. Sarah knew she wouldn't. Mama didn't notice things, didn't tell her what to do even when they lived in Detroit. When Sarah learned from some of the neighbors how to get electricity—steal electricity—from the pole in the back alley, Mama never told her not to do it. Now Mama was worse than ever, seemed to live in some fuzzy world all her own. She couldn't come out of that faraway place to live with Sarah.

Still, remembering what Uncle Marsh said to comfort her, Sarah could believe, as she had that first night, that everyone had come to welcome them, after all.

❧ 10 ❧

In the two weeks since they arrived, Keziah never said boo about hiding Daddy's undershirt for Sarah. There were a few days now and then when Sarah didn't have to wear it but kept it folded in the same highboy drawer, hidden under Grandmama's handkerchiefs. The smell had begun to fade, the odor of Daddy's sweat and last blood. Sometimes it smelled so much like her own smell that she couldn't remember which part was Daddy. And now the shirt held some of the fragrance of Grandmama's room, too.

Keziah came every morning, right up the front walk, not around to the back the way Nancy's Thelma did. Once in a while, when someone came up to get her with some new story about her mother, Keziah had to go home in the middle of the day to take care of Aunt Sude. Sometimes Aunt Sude got mean and insulted some of the neighbors so seriously that Keziah's presence was required at home, they said. Keziah never slept during the day on anyone's bed the way Thelma did, but sometimes, chewing on a thorn from a locust tree, she stood inside the front door screen and watched people walk up the street and back. Sometimes she spoke to them and sometimes she didn't, just according to who they were. Keziah and Mama both nodded and waved to a tall, thin boy who walked by the house nearly every day. And he nodded and waved back. Mama said he was a nice boy. She had known his father once a long time ago, she said, and Sarah did not like the way Mama kind of prissied around when the boy appeared. His last name was Daniells. Now he lived down Laurel Street with his grandmother, just for the summer.

Uncle Marsh had to go over to Knoxville often. He went over to talk to people about the Tennessee River being flooded, about how they felt when what was their farmland became river bottom. This was, he told Sarah, the result of one of those alphabet programs the Government developed to help bring cheap electricity to this part of the country. He called the project the TVA for Tennessee Valley Authority, he said, but Mama told her that some people thought it was pure, unadulterated socialism come to the USA.

"Some people will lose their farms," he said. "Some their homes. But then they'll get lights and radios and washing machines."

Sarah tried to imagine what it would be like not to have lights on when you came home in the dark or a radio to listen to after you went to bed, or to wash all your clothes by hand in the river, maybe. It would be hard to choose between your home and electricity. When Uncle Marsh told her about the old man sitting on his front porch all night, night after night, with his rifle cocked and ready across his knees, ready to shoot the men who came to take him off his land, she remembered the morning she left her house, her little room under the eaves. She wished then that she had taken Daddy's rifle the way the old farmer did and waited on the porch, the gun cocked and ready, while she still had the chance.

Keziah had carried the potted fern they brought with them from Detroit into the house that first night and put it in Uncle Marsh's bedroom, just off the living room. It grew greener and bushier under her careful tending, and pretty soon Sarah noticed pale green, curled fingers reaching up from the dirt in the pot. Mama forgot all about the Mrs. Herbert Hoover rose and how she made Sarah ride all the way with the rose crowding her out of the backseat, but Keziah watered it, even put a fish head in the hole when she replanted it outside. No matter, it withered and died. Sarah knew it would.

"Things don't like to be transplanted a million miles from home," she said.

"How's come that fern still lives, huh?" Keziah said. "That rose—too stuck up to change, that's all."

Sarah knew Keziah was really talking about her, but she couldn't change. She longed to see a movie on a Saturday morning at the Riviera with its starry ceiling, longed to look at the paintings at the new art museum. But most of all, she missed Nancy and their walks to school. School here in Hanlon would be out in just a few weeks and Mama said there wasn't any point in starting so late in the term. Sarah tried not to think about the fall.

Also in those first weeks, Keziah made Sarah help her with

the work. On washdays Sarah carried heavy wash baskets up stone steps from the basement, outdoors to the side yard for Keziah. While they folded wet sheets to hang on the line, Sarah handed her the clothespins, which Keziah held in her mouth. Why she, Sarah, had to do all the work while Mama didn't do a blessed thing but sleep was a mystery to Sarah.

About supper time, Keziah would hand Sarah a basket of early peas to shell. Sarah liked hearing the rattle-clatter of the peas as they rolled into the granite bowl, liked tasting their pungent greenness, like water. She worked with Keziah without speaking and sometimes watched Keziah make beaten biscuit on the shining metal machine built just for making those thin, crusty biscuits. When Keziah wasn't looking, Sarah tried to walk the way she did, but her hip-bones wouldn't move the right way nor could she stand up as straight. Sometimes when she spent the whole day with Keziah, she'd forget to think about Daddy, forget the words Mrs. Drisdon had warned her with. But most of the time she wanted her father to come walking up the front walk with his thumbs in his suspenders, walking on the balls of his feet and wearing a hat like Uncle Marsh did. It was a dream, a waking dream she held close each day.

"Honey, I forgot." Uncle Marsh called Sarah from the newspaper office one day to say he'd forgotten some notes for an article he was working on.

"Never mind, I'll bring them up to you," she said.

"It looks a lot like rain so just wait it out if it does. I'm in no hurry," he said.

Sarah walked up Central Street carrying the notes when she saw the man walking ahead of her with a familiar, unmistakable way of walking. It was someone she knew as well as she knew herself. Someone. . . . Her heart stopped for a moment and then beat so harshly she could feel it in her hands. *It had to be! It was. It was Daddy!* She ran, slowly at first, hesitating between steps. Then, when she was sure, she ran as fast as she had ever been able to run in her life. *To catch him. To take his hand! To bring him back to Mama, whole and unhurt!* She was so full of joy she couldn't breathe or speak. He turned a corner. She couldn't shout at him but ran faster than before. He walked like Daddy, straight-backed and elegant. Like a movie star, Mama said, though she never said which one. Now Sarah was close enough to touch him. She reached out. He turned to stare at her and mouthed words she did not hear; she saw only the opening and closing of his mouth, the gap between his yellowed front teeth, nothing like Daddy's.

Just as the first raindrops dotted the sidewalk in front of her, he turned in at the drugstore. She slumped against the brick wall of the store trying to get her breath. Of course it wasn't Daddy. It couldn't be. Why had she thought it would be? Why had she tried to live the dream? Entering the drugstore, she stood close to him at the cigarette counter, trying to hold onto the feeling a little longer. When he glared at her, she turned away. He left the drugstore then with his cigarettes, moved along First Street, swinging his arms.

Sarah stood in the doorway a moment, watching him go away through the rain and mist rising from the warm sidewalk. If she never gave up on her belief that Daddy was not dead and gone forever, she wondered, maybe he really would come back and start all over again. Maybe the next time, she thought, maybe next time.

With this new thought running around in her mind as if it were looking for a place to settle, Sarah went back into the drugstore. By this time rain outside pelted down hard and warm so she sat down on a leatherette-covered stool to wait. When she asked Mr. Wolf, the pharmacist who sometimes worked behind the soda fountain, to fix her a Coca-Cola, her voice shook. Mr. Wolf didn't seem to notice. He scooped crushed ice into a glass, pushed the levers for Coca-Cola syrup and soda water while she put both sweaty hands flat on the cool marble counter and twisted herself back and forth on the revolving stool. She wanted to put her face, which was hot and red, onto the cool surface. Instead she watched herself, her eyes wide and staring, in the square mirror behind the fountain.

The same wave of sorrow she felt at Daddy's funeral washed over her again. She couldn't forget the idea that her father might be walking around town still alive and not deep in a coffin in the ground back in Detroit. She wasn't sure she even wanted to forget. Uncle Marsh had said her grief would heal in time, but she was certain now she would never get over it.

She thought that by looking away from her own image in the mirror framed with ornate wood carvings of leaves and flowers all round, she could keep herself from crying. However, someone else's face had come into view, close to hers. She didn't want anyone to see her now; she was still trembling and close to tears. But this was the face of the tall, thin boy who walked by their house each day, the boy Mama waved to, acting as if she knew him. He was seated now in a booth opposite her looking into the mirror at her. She closed her eyes, wishing he would disappear. She

60

didn't know how long he'd been there but hoped it wasn't long enough to see her reach out to the unknown man. Suddenly the boy puffed out his cheeks as if he were blowing up a balloon and kept making that face at her until she had to smile.

Mr. Wolf brought her Coke and she breathed in its strong, sweet smell. She reached for a straw in the tall glass container. Someone had packed them so tightly that she had to give the lid an extra jerk to lift the straws up. When she did that, all the straws, every last one, squirted out of the jar and fell onto the floor like a giant game of Pick-Up-Sticks. She tried to pretend that it hadn't happened, swept one or two straws off the counter with her arm and hoped no one noticed. As she brushed the paper straws away, she tipped her Coke over and the brown liquid seeped toward Uncle Marsh's notes. She grabbed them.

Mr. Wolf laughed at her and picked up a damp rag. "Hurry up," he said. "I'll get the Coke. You pick up them straws, missy, 'fore somebody comes in here and sees this mess. What they don't know won't hurt them, you get my meaning?"

Still holding Uncle Marsh's papers, Sarah slid off the stool. The boy knelt beside her, handed her the straws, one by one. She felt her face flush hot and red again. "You always this sloppy?" He smiled when he said it.

"No," she said and then something, some bravado she didn't know she had, especially where boys were concerned, made her add, "Worse. You should see me when I'm not out in public."

He stood up. "Better not use a straw around here." He brushed off his hands against his khaki-colored trousers.

"Not for a while, anyhow. Why don't you sit over in the booth with me?"

So, while Mr. Wolf cleaned off the counter and packed the straws back into the container, Sarah put Uncle Marsh's notes on the seat and sat down. She told him she was Sarah Raines.

"I live with my Uncle Marsh Stannard," she said.

"Yeah, I know."

". . . my mother and I . . ."

"Yeah." He nodded.

"You know?"

"Sure. You live in a small town, everybody knows everybody else. Period. It's a fact."

"Well, I guess so," she said. And she remembered that she already knew he lived with his grandmother for the summer.

"What's your name?" Sarah felt like a fool, as if she were asking some child, "What's your name, little boy?" But he answered with the same politeness she'd found in everyone here in Kentucky.

"I'm Peter Daniells," he said. "I'm going to Centre College in the fall, but right now . . . right now, I have to stay here."

His voice trailed off to nothingness as if there were something on his mind he couldn't talk about any more than she could talk about her father's terrible secret. She wondered briefly what his secret might be and if he knew anything about hers.

"I'm going back up to my grandmother's. Want to walk along?" he said. He stood up and she looked directly at him for the first time. His eyes were green behind his glasses, as green as Uncle Marsh's.

They went out into the rain, turning toward Laurel Street.

Sarah didn't believe she actually could walk down the street with him without any of her usual shyness, without acting tongue-tied, as Nancy put it whenever boys were around. "What's the matter, the cat got your tongue?" she'd say in one of her mean moods.

They walked along the sidewalk together past the hospital, past the school. Peter said his father had gone there and Sarah smiled because her mother had gone there, too. The rain, like someone crying, stopped and the sun came out. And then, she didn't know why, perhaps it was something in the way he squinted at her through his glasses as if everything she said was important and he didn't want to miss a word, she began to talk. She told him about how she followed the man who looked like her father, about how she reached out to him. She said she thought her father was alive then and whole—as if a dream had come to life, like in a moving picture, maybe. She told him about eating Mama's canned tomatoes for breakfast sometimes and about not going to school since Daddy's funeral. She did not tell him about the way Daddy used his brother's gun on himself.

Still, she talked and talked more than she ever had to Nancy even, or Uncle Marsh. She did not know why. Peter was not what Nancy would consider handsome. He didn't look like any famous movie stars they yearned over on the pages of movie magazines. Looking like a glamorous star was one of Nancy's requirements for boys, and Nancy knew more about boys than Sarah did. Peter had those glasses and plain brown hair; yet there was his quiet attention, the way he said "What did you do then?" or "Honest?" and the way he turned around in front of her and walked backward, facing her, listening.

They reached her front gate. They were quiet for a moment and Sarah remembered something Keziah had said.

"It seems like you can talk to a stranger sometimes better'n you can talk to the closest one to you. Like in a bus depot or the train station? You can just set there and blurt out everything you know to some old soul you know you're never goin' see again in this world."

"Want to come in?" Sarah said, feeling the closeness, "and sit on the porch awhile?" But before she said "iced tea" he said no, he had to meet a girl up on Laurel Hill later on.

Sarah remembered Uncle Marsh's papers when she heard the first ring of the telephone bell inside the house. Without answering it, she ran back toward the drugstore.

Sarah hoped with all her heart she would never have to see Peter Daniells again.

11

Sarah didn't tell Mama anything about meeting Peter nor did she mention it to Keziah the next morning when they cleaned upstairs. They were in Mama's room, the room she'd left when she eloped with Daddy, Keziah told her.

"Everything," Keziah said, "right down to the las' pin— left exactly like it was."

"That bone-handled brush set you see there?" Keziah pointed to a marble-topped dresser. "Your mama got that for her birthday. Eighteen, she was, three weeks to the day 'fore she skedaddled down them steps with your daddy. Yessiree, he marched himself up here. Came right *in* here and got her. Took her away while your grandmammy sat there readin' day in and day out. Read! All that woman ever did do. . . ." She shook her head. "And your grandpappy? It killed him too," she said. "Purely killed them both. All them pretty things? All they ever did do after that was set here and turn yellow."

On the dresser with the brush and comb was a small,

round holder to match. Through the hole in the top, Sarah saw a coil of hair.

"For hair combin's. Don't you know nuthin'? That's your Mama's own red hair, child. Miz Stannard, she believed you can't throw away anybody's hair cuttin's. They'll die, sure as you do," Keziah said.

Sarah left the hair where it was, and Mrs. Drisdon's face swam in place of Keziah's for a moment.

"I don't think anyone has been in here for years," was all she could think of to say.

"You right about that. Only me. Myself. Clean in the spring, all by myself." Keziah sniffed and wiped her nose with the back of her hand.

Yes, Keziah and Sarah and Uncle Marsh worked while Mama didn't do much of anything except sleep her life away. No more tending her roses or canning tomatoes and doing her embroidery. Even if Keziah hadn't done all the work, Sarah was certain that Mama would not have. She hadn't been doing anything much at home in Detroit after Daddy went away, only it was winter and there wasn't much to do. And it didn't matter much, either.

Sarah went into Granddaddy's room, which Mama had taken as her room. She was there now, asleep in the big wooden bed, curled like a child under too many bedclothes, her head hidden beneath feather pillows.

Keziah said, "I believe to my soul that woman has gone to collect the reward in heaven that she deserves."

Keziah put the yellowed mirror next to Mama's face to see, she said, if her breath misted the glass.

"That's how they check to see if a body is livin'!"

66

Mama woke up then, but just enough to smile at them and then turn over on her stomach to sleep some more.

Sarah finished her work and went downstairs to write to Nancy on Uncle Marsh's typewriter. She didn't want to look at Mama's sleep-puffed face any longer or worry about what was going to become of her.

Dear Nancy,

I bet you never thought you'd get a letter from me every day, did you? Thanks for all yours. I still haven't met anyone my age except that boy Peter I told you about. He usually comes by every day but I haven't seen him lately. I think he has a girl friend—he's 17! You wouldn't like him. He doesn't look like Clark Gable. Is he still your favorite?

Uncle Marsh and Miss Bennet are going to think of some places to take me. She belongs to the Book-of-the-Month Club and she brings me her books. Mama doesn't like to see me ruin my eyes sitting around reading all day. But I loved *The Good Earth*. Have you read it yet? Or will your mother let you?

I play the Victrola here a lot but the only records we have are Sir Harry Lauder. He sings silly Scottish songs. And Enrico Caruso. He's that tenor, you know, from Italy and my mother likes him. My mother likes him a lot. She got up yesterday and made some rose sugar. She never did that at home. She buried a new rose in a jar of sugar. Then she'll put it in her iced tea. The sugar, that is. I hope there aren't any ants in it! Ha! Ha!

You'd really like the house we live in now. It is even

bigger than yours. It is on the side of a hill, Laurel Hill, but it looks like a mountain to me. There is a little gravel path leading down the hill to the street in back of our house where Miss Bennet (she's a teacher here) lives in Uncle Marsh's little house. My grandfather built it for U. M. to live in when he came back home after he got wounded in the war. My mother calls it the "honeymoon cottage," only it never was.

Thank goodness I am not going to school here. The school building has wooden floors, if you can imagine it! Like Kern's Department Store. It makes a terrible noise when people walk on it. It is so old, my mother went there and some of her teachers are still there. Ugh! Did I tell you Peter Daniells' father went there? I am planning on coming back to Detroit this fall, so maybe I won't have to go to school here at all. I hope!

Their picture show has wooden floors, too, and is not beautiful like the Riviera Theater.

I saw "Forty-Second Street" again. My favorite movie, I think. I went with Uncle Marsh and we sat in the projection booth with the man who owns the movie. We didn't have to pay and guess what? I drank beer!!! We rubbed salt on a glass and then we drank the beer. Don't tell your mother but you can tell Thelma if you want to. Uncle Marsh said not to tell mine either. We used the same glass. I drank out of one side and he drank out of the other.

Sometimes I go to his newspaper office with him and he lets me put type in the big linotype machine for him. He makes me a printer's devil hat out of newspaper and lets me say h--- and d---.

No, Keziah is not our maid. My mother said she is not. And she is my only friend. I have a second cousin here who is 17 but she is visiting in Louisville and I haven't met her.

Well, I must close now. Keziah wants me to set the table. See why she is not a maid?

Sincerely yours,
Sarah Stannard Raines

P.S. I'll tell you if I meet Peter D. again.

Mr. Cooper came up on the front porch every day to pick up Sarah's daily letter to Nancy and to deliver fat, pink envelopes with messages to Sarah in Nancy's curling, round handwriting on the back. Mama got letters, too, but she never opened the mail the minute she got it. Sarah couldn't understand how she could let a letter lie unopened on the hall table right where Mr. Cooper left it. Sometimes Sarah brought the pearl-handled letter opener out for Mama to use when the spirit moved her, as Keziah put it. When there was an envelope from Mrs. Drisdon, Sarah wanted Mama to read it right away.

"Did she say she found renters for us, Mama?"

"Well, read it for yourself, honey. She says that brother of hers—Sam?—might want . . . but she's said that before."

Often, Mama would leave the letter on the porch for days. Once, when another letter came about the house, Mama said, "The way Miz Drisdon keeps after me to rent the house for next to nothing reminds me of the way she offered to drive us to the cemetery and back and then asked me to pay for the gas!"

Mama couldn't make up her mind whether to sell or rent, and Sarah longed to write her own letter to Mrs. Drisdon refusing all her offers, so she could get back home. But Mama just sat there on the front porch every nice day and wouldn't write to Mrs. Drisdon or go over to Knoxville with Uncle Marsh or help Keziah or anything. All she wanted to do was swing and sip iced tea. When Keziah brought her the drinks on a tray, she'd set the tray on the table just out of Mama's reach so Mama would have to stop the swing and get up and go over to get the tea glass.

When it wasn't nice enough for Mama to sit outside, she'd wander through the house as if she was looking for something she'd lost. She'd stop at the piano, maybe, and pick out songs with one finger as Sarah watched from the window seat where she read the books Miss Bennet lent her. Mama didn't sit down to play but stood up and leaned over the bench, as though she was too busy to stop what she was doing but needed to hear some tune.

"All alone, I'm so all alone . . .
Waiting for a ring, a ting-a-ling."

"Don't you know no happy songs?" Keziah came into the living room every time, usually with flour on her arms. "And, if you do, for the Lord's sweet sake, play one!" she'd say.

Then Mama would sit down on the bench and put her feet on all the pedals and play with both hands and feet. She'd play "Brother Can You Spare a Dime" and "Minnie the Moocher" until Keziah in the back of the house laughed out loud.

The Block twins came through the side yard from next door nearly every day. Mama didn't mind about them com-

70

ing because she didn't have to talk. They did it all. The two maiden ladies with their thin gray hair and large pink moles on their faces in identical places were the oldest residents of Hanlon County. Uncle Marsh said they recollected firsthand what it was like to live here when mules sank to their bellies in mud on Front Street.

"The twins," he said, "think of themselves as one by now. I do not believe they know their own given names."

Today, when they came through the wide place they'd made in the hedge, Mama was in her usual place on the swing. She still wore her bathrobe, which, until they came to Hanlon, Sarah had only seen hanging on a hook in her bedroom closet at home.

"Hoo hoo," the twins sang out in unison. "Miz Raines? Oh, there you are. We come to tell you the news. . ."

". . . about Miz Satterlee's latest baby?"

Sarah saw them from her place in Uncle Marsh's room where she typed another letter to Nancy. Mama fanned herself with the oval palm leaf fan from the funeral parlor.

The twins were deaf in the same degree. They seemed to have that in common just as they had everything else.

"They told her, poor thing, at the hospital?"

". . . told her the newest baby was a boy. But then they changed their minds!"

". . . now mind, Miz Raines, this is a secret, so don't you whisper it to a soul."

The twins spoke in voices loud enough to be heard by anyone on the sidewalk.

". . . certain parts. You get our meaning?"

". . . certain parts were on the inside instead of the out!"

They paused. Sarah sat up in her chair.

71

". . . or, sister, was it the other way around?"

". . . had to take it, whichever it was, over to Louisville to those fine doctors over there."

Sarah put down her pen, wiped off the point with a little ink-stained cloth. She wondered what Mrs. Satterlee and her baby would say if they could hear what the twins were saying. Spreading its secret all over town, they were. Her heart beat a little faster. It was unforgivable to tell someone's secret.

Then, without skipping a beat of the rhythm of their loud talk, the Block twins asked Mama, so that everyone could hear, why her husband killed himself with his own brother's gun that way.

❧ 12 ❧

Sarah sat very still for a moment, letting the words flow over her like scalding liquid. She crumpled the paper on which she'd been writing to Nancy about Uncle Marsh's newspaper, held it in her hand, trying to squeeze the words off the paper where they landed.

"It is hard to say," she heard Mama's polite voice. She spoke loud enough for the twins to hear. Why didn't she chase them home? Why didn't she tell them it was all lies, to take their sickening stories and their stolen secrets and go back where they came from? Why was Mama shouting, too?

"He, uh, he wasn't working, you see? No job? He was . . . proud?"

Mama spoke as if to children. Sarah tried to remember what Mrs. Drisdon had told her, tried to say the words over to herself, but they wouldn't come. How did the twins know? Who had told them?

"Everyone knows!" she said to herself. She still stood in the center of the bedroom. For some reason, she thought about Peter. *He knows, too.* She held onto the warm cloth of Daddy's undershirt beneath her blouse. But it didn't help. She couldn't do it all, not any more. Lights burst behind her eyes. She couldn't hold back the tears any longer.

Throwing herself against the screen door, she stumbled outside, pounding the air with clenched fists. Mama half stood up, lifted herself out of the swing. The twins did not move, hearing only their own voices. Mama was all the way up now, and as she rose, the pressure in Sarah's head seemed to turn red and burst wide open. She couldn't stop herself now. She jumped up and down in a frenzied dance of fury. Mama stared at her. Keziah, out in the garden, knelt in the dirt, a white rag around her head.

"You told! Uncle Marsh told! Them. . . ." Sarah threw her arm toward the two old women. Screaming, she fell against the wall.

"How could you? He didn't! He didn't! He didn't!"

Oh, didn't they know her father would never do such a thing? Leave her alone like that, leave her to wonder? It was all a lie.

A ramshackle car pulled up to the curb. Sarah shook her head and her arms at a woman inside the car, her face blurred behind the glass. Mr. Cooper, carrying his leather bag filled with mail, stood on the other side of the street looking down at letters in his hand. Everything had stopped except her own fury.

Sarah leaned against the porch column and sobbed into the milky paint. Mama drew closer and she knew Mama was going to touch her.

"Don't. Don't touch me. Stay away. It is all your fault,

bringing me here. I need. . . ." She could not say what she needed.

"Oh, Lord, Sarah. What is it? Stop now, honey." Mama touched her now.

Sarah hit at Mama's arm, her face, anything. She felt like a lunatic, like the crazy Raines she was. Isn't that what Mama said she was? She couldn't stop. Daddy's undershirt came untucked and she twisted it around and around her cold fingers.

"Stop, Sarah," Mama said. "Everybody in town's going to hear."

"Who cares? Everybody knows anyway!"

And then Mama slapped her. Sarah stopped flailing her arms, stopped dancing up and down.

"You get inside, young lady." Mama looked at Sarah as if she'd never seen her before. "And, Lord have mercy, what on earth is that filthy thing you are wearing?"

The twins, by this time, were across the side yard, stepping close together like chorus dancers in a line on the stage. Keziah had disappeared and Mr. Cooper climbed the narrow steps of the house across the street. Sarah gasped. She felt the way she did when she had scarlet fever and pneumonia at the same time.

"Get to your room."

Sarah wanted to stop breathing, feeling anything. She tried to imagine what it was like to die. What would it be like when everything stopped, even the jumble of her own thoughts? She pictured her blood threading through veins, up and down her legs and into her fingers. She willed it to stop. She wanted to be like ice in a stream, freezing to the bottom of everything.

75

She wanted to get into her bed, Grandmama's bed and be left alone, but Mama followed her in and shut the door. Her voice came in hard spurts, like slaps.

"I cannot stand this, Sarah! I can't stand any more! First him. And now you! Mercy! Mercy!"

"Mama, don't. Please. I tried. Honest, I tried."

"You'd think, wouldn't you, that you'd want to be some kind of comfort to me? We'd be comfort to each . . . but, no. You carry on like a banshee. You're just like your Aunt Wanda Raines. Crazy. All of 'em, crazy!"

Sarah put her hands over her ears.

"Papa was right, you know," Mama said. "He said they're all crazy." Mama held onto the end of the bed, her hands wrapped around the bar, her knuckles yellow and white. "You listen to me, now." She pulled at Sarah's hands. "Now I'm going to have another one! That's what I want you to know, Miss Sarah Stannard Raines!"

Mama let go of Sarah's hands and walked over to the door. "You can't hide from me. You've got to know sometime. You are going to be a big sister."

Sarah didn't recognize her own voice when she spoke. It was an old, old woman's voice. "I wish," she said, "I wish you were dead. I wish it was you and not him."

☙ 13 ☙

There was a knock on Sarah's bedroom door. Without waiting for an answer, Keziah came right in. She towered over Sarah like a tree, all six feet of her, her hands on her hips.

"You know you been stove up here two whole days? It's time," she said, "it is way past time for you to come back to the land of the livin'. You might as well get this straight in your mind, girl. I ain't bringin' no more food in here."

Keziah moved around the room as she talked. She snapped window shades until they rolled up noisily, closed dresser drawers, leaving little tag ends of clothing sticking out. She tilted the mirror upright so Sarah could see herself, her hair a rats' nest, as Mama put it, her face gray, eyes staring out like someone afraid.

". . . sick and tired of bein' the only one 'round here got any get up and go. I got it all to do here. You and her . . ." —Keziah jerked a thumb toward Mama's room—"hidin' in the bed!"

Keziah pointed a long finger at Sarah. "Beans is way late.

77

Right kind of moon tonight. You goin' be out there in the garden this very mornin' down on your hands and knees. Throwin' a fit's one thing. Lazy's another. Now you get up from there and make that bed."

With Keziah on the outside and Sarah on the wall side of the bed, they smoothed sheets, plumped pillows, arranged the tasseled spread over the quilt. Sarah thought about all the times that Keziah had made someone else's bed and knew if they wet the bed after they were grown. Keziah knew a whole lot more about them than they knew about her.

"It's botherin' your mama. She feelin' bad about how she told you the news," Keziah said with the pillow under her chin.

"I don't care."

"If you didn't care, you wouldn't be sittin' here rockin'. Come on now, you and your mama make up so you can belong to one another again."

Sarah plumped up her pillow and thought about how she, and now the new baby, belonged to Mama. She wondered if the baby could hear all the words that had been said, the tears that had been shed since its life began, and if it would know that no one wanted it to be born.

She found packages of seed on a wooden bench against the basement wall. Keziah saved them year after year, she said: the meatiest tomatoes, slices as big as a dinner plate, the sweetest peas, the fattest limas.

"Generations unto the future," Keziah said.

There were paper sacks filled with black wax bean seeds, cinnamon-colored green beans, spinach no bigger than a period in a sentence, wrinkled pale peas, and papery onion sets to be set out in the second planting of the year. Sarah looked at the seeds and thought they were like the baby, known but not known.

"Keziah, you reckon Mama's baby'll have red hair like she does? Or black like me . . . and my father?"

"Time'll tell. Don't count your chickens. . . ."

"Yes, but black seeds make yellow beans, so the baby could have yellow or brown hair, maybe."

"How come you to ask me such a thing as that?"

"I don't know. I wondered is all. Thinking about the baby and how it might look."

Keziah didn't say any more. Sarah guessed she didn't know what the baby would be like, either. Instead Keziah got down on her hands and knees in the dirt and ran one finger along the row already marked with a string. She dropped the beans, one by one, into the trough. She covered them with dirt and then stood up, resting her hand, pink palm out, on her hip.

"Go ask your mama," she said finally. "She the one with the learnin'. Not me."

They were quiet then, working together, planting the seeds, smoothing the earth, their shoulders touching. Sun warmed Sarah's back as she stretched her arms above her head. She stopped thinking about the baby. She didn't have to think about anything, working in a garden. Now she knew why Daddy liked digging in the garden. It was like breathing. You just had to take a little stick or your finger, make a long trough in the earth, and then kneel down to thumb seeds in, one by one.

Keziah disappeared and pretty soon here came Mama out into the yard to work, too. She knelt down and put both hands in the dirt and crumbled it up, letting it fall into her skirt. Mama's face was hidden beneath a wide-brimmed straw hat and her voice came out of it as if from far away.

"It seems that we have misunderstood each other once again." She crumbled some more dirt. "I wish I . . . I don't believe that we do this on purpose. I wish I could start over. Honestly, Sarah. I am going to do better."

❧ 14 ❧

A few days later, she met her Aunt Wanda Raines for the first time. When she saw her, Sarah knew exactly what she'd look like when she herself was old. She'd had the same queer sense of recognition when she first met Uncle Marsh. How was it possible to see herself in Aunt Wanda when the Raineses and the Stannards were so different? Still, it was true. Sarah saw her father's face and her own reflected in Aunt Wanda Raines' high cheekbones and deep-set eyes, her long chin.

Aunt Wanda Raines came up on the front porch early, before Mama was out of bed. The sun hadn't cleared the top of Big Black mountain but slanted long, yellow rays through openings between smaller hills to light the dusty street. Tiny dust motes swam in the sunshine as Sarah sat in her mother's place on the swing. She could swing high enough to touch the ceiling with bare toes, and this was easy to do as long as Keziah didn't catch her.

At first the woman looked like any of the mountain women

who came into town bringing bags of poke sallet greens cut from the roadsides or berries they'd picked and put into lard buckets. They came into town to sell their garden truck because their husbands weren't working in the coal mines or anywhere else. She wore a print dress and a man's fedora hat on her head. Her face was wrinkled. Deep wrinkles like dry cracks in hard-baked earth lined her face, and her light-blue eyes were faded and deep behind round, heavy cheekbones. She was big, deep-chested, and strong, Sarah saw, almost like a man.

"Sarah?"

Sarah stopped the swing by putting both feet flat on the floor and almost catapulted herself into the woman's path. They were of the same height, and Sarah could look directly into her eyes. Whenever she stood next to Mama, Mama would rise up taller than she usually was and stand on tiptoes sometimes. Now it was Sarah who stood up as tall as she could. It was then that she knew this was her father's only living sister, crazy Aunt Wanda Raines herself. She didn't look crazy to Sarah, just hot and dusty.

"Sarah?" She said it again in a rough, deep voice. It sounded like "Surah."

"You know my name?"

"I'd know ye anywhere." In a lower voice she added, "Sarah's my own mother's name. Your daddy, bless his heart, gave it to you."

Sarah didn't know what to say. She'd never known before that it was her daddy who named her. She looked down at the woman's feet. Aunt Wanda Raines wore men's shoes. Sarah felt another unexpected kinship with her. Sarah had worn Mrs. Drisdon's old blue oxfords, two sizes too big, for

82

so long herself. Aunt Wanda Raines sat down abruptly on the top step and Sarah sat down beside her, watching every move she made. Aunt Wanda drew her knees up to her chest and covered her knees with her dress. Without thinking, Sarah did the same thing.

Sarah sat close enough to catch Aunt Wanda's smell. She smelled different from anyone Sarah had ever smelled before—strong, peppery, sharp, making her nose wrinkle. Somehow it was a good smell, and Sarah moved closer. Aunt Wanda didn't seem to know she smelled that way—of sun on wooden boards and green things, and that other aroma steaming out from her lean body. Sweat, it was. Mama certainly never smelled that way. Mama smelled of lavender sachet and clean clothes and canned tomatoes and feather pillows—that is, when she let Sarah get close enough to smell her.

"I been studyin' a way to get over here to see you. Your Uncle Marshall Stannard . . . he thought we'd like to meet. Never set eyes on ye a'fore now and, well, sir . . . you are your father's child."

She went on. "It's a wise child that knows its own father. The Bible says that, did ye know it?"

Aunt Wanda looked at Sarah so long that she had to look away. Her light-blue eyes seemed to see everything about Sarah, things that Sarah didn't want known to this strange woman. Aunt Wanda Raines slapped her long hand on her thigh and an odor of crushed raspberries flew up.

"Laaaw! You are a sight for sore eyes. By the by, I'm sister to your Daddy, livin' up on the Poor Fork Road, way up yonder." She stuck her hand out and Sarah took it in hers.

"Livin' alone. Mammy and Pap dead and in the grave. All

the brothers gone, two in the war and one bein' your daddy. Bet ye didn't know that, did ye? You 'n me, we're the only ones left to tell the tale."

"Yes'm."

Watching Aunt Wanda Raines was the next best thing to watching the Saturday afternoon movie serial. You never knew what was going to happen next.

Aunt Wanda stood up almost as fast as she sat down.

"Bein' as I already been this far, I reckon I'll just go on over yonder to the store. I don't reckon you'd care to come on up and see me, would ye? I'll be expectin' ye!"

Later, when Mama got out of bed and Sarah told her about Aunt Wanda's invitation, both Keziah and Mama said no, Sarah wasn't going traipsing up the mountain to spend any time with *that* woman. But Uncle Marsh said Aunt Wanda was about as crazy as old Judge Jefferson Davis Harte and Dr. Spidell all rolled into one. And it was Uncle Marsh who made Mama let her go and told Keziah not to be so stuck up and then drove Sarah up the Poor Fork Road to find Aunt Wanda's house. He was on his way to Pineville, and it was early morning. Fingers of fog lay in the hollows, waiting to cling to morning sun and burn away. Heat lightning flicked across ridges in the distance and, up close, wisps of smoke rose from stone chimneys of houses perched along the road-side. There was the smell of coal smoke and sun, mists rising.

On the drive up the mountain and out of town, Uncle Marsh told her about how they needed new roads so people could get their garden truck and handmade furniture to flatland markets. Sarah could have spent the rest of her life just sitting beside him, listening to him talk, riding, riding along forever. She wanted to say, "I love you and I want to stay with you," but she was afraid he would close his eyes the way he did sometimes and forget people were there.

"I certainly do wish your mama had come along," he said. "Looks like we are going to have to take her in hand, aren't we?"

"Yes, sir." Sarah *didn't* want Mama there, but she knew that Uncle Marsh was worried about the way Mama stayed in bed so much.

"Well, I guess we have to give her a little time."

Down in the valley below them, pale sun touched galvanized tin roofs, and they glittered through the mist. They had come to a little hollow rising up between two ridges. Uncle Marsh slowed the car.

"I'll drop you here," he said.

"Smoke's coming out of her chimney; that's her house. She'll be expectin' you."

Sarah changed her mind about spending the day with Aunt Wanda Raines and maybe the night, too, if Uncle Marsh couldn't get back before dark. This place was deserted. Back home in Detroit, when she'd gone to call on friends, there were numbers on the houses and black-and-white street signs tacked to light poles at the corner. There were telephones in most houses where you were invited to stay the night.

"Honey, just slip out of the car." Uncle Marsh almost pushed her out of the car onto the roadside. She pressed back against the seat and slumped down out of sight, she hoped.

"Go on, Sarah. Go on down to her door. I'll turn the car around way up there and come back down. And I'll see you at suppertime or maybe tomorrow morning. Tell Miz Raines 'hello' for me."

He reached across Sarah and opened the door. She stepped out of the car, carrying her little bundle of night-clothes. She felt as though he'd dropped her into a deep hole.

"You just wave now, you hear?"

He was truly trying to get rid of her, she thought as she looked at the house. She remembered Mama warning her about Uncle Marsh, how he took people on as a cause and then dropped them when, Mama said, his ardor cooled.

"First there was Anna, the one Papa built the Honeymoon Cottage for—he stayed in France after the war and she finally had to marry someone else. Before that there was that intense friendship with the son of one of Papa's Hungarian miners," Mama said. "Marsh practically lived in the coal camp with them one summer. Teachin' the family English, spending the night. Why, he even got head lice up there. And then—it always happens—his enthusiasm faded and he went off to Kansas or someplace on the railroad. When he finally came back, the family had moved to the coalfields in West Virginia."

So Sarah turned toward the house, which was as close to the dirt road as it could be without being right on the road. There wasn't even one step up onto the long porch stretched across the front of the house, held up from the hard-packed dirt yard by flat stones at each corner. It all seemed to grow right out of the road and down the hill in the back. On the unpainted porch railing, lard buckets bloomed with ivy, ge-ranium, and plants Sarah had never seen before. Vines grew everywhere, climbed on strings, shaded the porch furnished with a wood-slat swing and one straight-backed chair

86

propped against the wall. Sun glinted on the silvery lard cans, making little blossoms of light in Sarah's eyes. Lined up on every windowsill were bottles of every shape and size you could imagine, blue, green, red and yellow bottles drawing in light from the low sun.

Sarah heard Uncle Marsh's car straining up the high road, backing and filling to turn around. Everything else was quiet. Aunt Wanda Raines was nowhere in sight. She still had time to run back to the road, wave Uncle Marsh down, and go on over to Pineville with him.

"Come right on in, Sarah. I'm in here. Fixin' us something to break the fast of the night." Aunt Wanda's voice came out of the half-opened door.

When Aunt Wanda came out onto the porch, she stopped in a rainbow patch on the floor. She looked as if she had one purple eye and one yellow. She wore a crown of leaves on her head. Tied across her forehead and pointing down over her face and into her eyes, leaves stood at crazy angles and twined in her coal-black hair. Maybe Mama was right, after all. Sarah looked back at the road. Uncle Marsh was there. He leaned out and waved.

"Bye, Sarah. See you when I see you. Howdy, Miz Raines."

He sped away with his tires spattering gravel, and she was stuck there with crazy Aunt Wanda Raines and her hat of leaves for the whole day and maybe even the whole night.

❧ 15 ❧

"It's just a Christian joy to me you're here. If the facts be known, I'm overjoyed." Aunt Wanda pointed to the leaves on her forehead. "What you see here, child, is beets."

"Beets," Sarah said.

"Yes'm, beets. Beet greens is the best hand to draw out a headache. In just a little while, honey, it'll be about gone."

She served Sarah bitter coffee made from chicory weed, she said, because she had no cash money for the real thing. The hot drink and thin, crusty corn bread spread with wild blackberry preserves—that's what they had for breakfast. Sarah ate, trying not to look at the beet leaves dangling in her Aunt's face. She sipped the bitter drink through her lips, letting it flow back hot into the corners of her mouth where she could really taste it. She liked it but was afraid she shouldn't. It was Mama standing right there looking at the beet leaves and the chicory, never noticing the vines and the bottles.

Aunt Wanda wore trousers, men's old pants bunched

around her waist and tied with a rope. Each time she moved, the heavy, woolen pants seemed to turn one way and her body another.

When Aunt Wanda struck a match against her big trousers and sucked in on her pipe, filling the room with thick, fragrant smoke, Sarah wondered what Mama would say. Somehow, a pipe was not the same as the cigarettes Uncle Marsh and Miss Bennet smoked so gracefully.

"I'm a-goin' to show you your bed for tonight," Aunt Wanda said. She laughed, showing yellow teeth, like a horse. She opened the door of a big Murphy bed to expose a mattress and wire springs.

"See, it opens up," she said, "and then kinda folds down and out of there. Like a tongue." Aunt Wanda stuck out her tongue, and Sarah had to laugh.

"Even got a Sunday quilt on it. Ain't nary a soul ever slept here. Once thought your Mammy and Daddy would. I wouldn't have it in mind to name me no names, but I reckon you'll be the first."

All day Aunt Wanda Raines led Sarah along mountain paths, down into little rocky gulleys and up narrow ridges, past shacks and the people living in them, all clinging to hills like spiders she thought.

"They been eatin' vi'let tops and wild greens so long, they're plumb green," her aunt said. Aunt Wanda cut a stick for herself, one for Sarah.

"For snakes. Copperheads and things." She used hers to point out plants good for eating and doctoring.

"That there's sheep sorrel," she said. "Makes mighty good soup if you've got ary butter 'er cream to put with it. If not, just 'taters 'n onions."

They picked big wads of blackberries, as Aunt Wanda put it, blackberries in brambles entangled in wild roses and unnamed weeds. Sarah heard birdsong she'd never heard before, and Aunt Wanda could name every one. Having only gray sparrows and a few robins in Detroit, Sarah couldn't imagine how Aunt Wanda memorized so many different songs.

Later, they found the remains of a moonshiner's still. Sarah never would have known the still was there, hidden as it was, in a low leafy room cut out of a laurel thicket. Aunt Wanda knew it was there, though, and she said some mountain families brewed whiskey in the woods like that because, she said, it was the best way they knew to make money from their crops of corn.

"Boys, they must have cleared out fast," Aunt Wanda laughed. "I reckon those revenuers found them up here farmin' in the woods!"

Sarah saw a ring of flat stones piled one atop the other and a trough of wood like a vine snaking down the hill, for water, Aunt Wanda said. She showed her a stick with a frazzled end to it like a big toothbrush. It smelled sour.

"Why do they have to hide their stills in the woods? We don't have Prohibition any more, do we?" Sarah knew the law against drinking and making whiskey was not in force anymore. President Roosevelt had made it all legal again. She remembered the arguments between her parents about it.

"Hunh! Moonshinin' will never die. Even with old Prohibition gone, trucks're still whining up these old roads ever' night. It's the taxes, girl." Aunt Wanda spat in the dirt.

Sarah had never seen a grown woman spit like that, right in front of someone else.

"A man's got to have a way to sell his corn," Aunt Wanda said and wiped her mouth with her hand. Sarah moved her mouth, tried to work up some spit, too. She couldn't let it go and decided it was Mama walking along right beside her, even in the deep woods.

When they got back to the cabin with bags full of greens and buckets of berries, bark for teas, and wild flowers, the sun had slipped behind the mountain so it looked like a half-circle of red. Uncle Marsh was not there waiting. Now that it was getting dark, Aunt Wanda, her house, and the dark hills seemed unfamiliar, strange to Sarah. Everything here was so different from Uncle Marsh's house with its tall windows and patterned carpets and graceful furniture. Here the porch vines clung and coiled like snakes now. Rainbows no longer poured out of colored bottles and the bottles seemed messy and untidy. Sarah listened for the scrunching sound Uncle Marsh's car would make against the gravel. The low ceiling pressed down on her and still Uncle Marsh did not come.

Aunt Wanda cooked some wild greens and made hot biscuit. They had buttermilk and wild berries for supper. Sarah looked for a dinner napkin at her plate, and when it wasn't there she thought of Mama again. Aunt Wanda put her elbows on the table and broke cold corn bread into her milk.

"They never was a man like yer daddy for wild greens," she said. "How he did love to set up after supper, sing or tell stories. Ye didn't know that, did ye?"

"Yes'm," Sarah said. "He sang. He and Mama, sometimes . . . when he wasn't. . . ." Sarah couldn't say "sick" the way Mama did and she wasn't going to say drunk either.

". . . when he didn't have the darkness in him?"

"Yes'm. When he didn't have the darkness in him."

Sarah thought that Aunt Wanda Raines could almost read her mind. Aunt Wanda told Sarah about the time that Harley and Lake, Daddy's brothers, went off to the war and John Andrew wasn't taken because of his rheumy heart. "Like to broke his pore old heart." Then John Andrew had it to do all alone, she said, "all the butchering, curing of hams, and planting things by moon signs, plowing, and working in the mines for cash."

It grew darker in the cabin and hotter from the coal stove. "Your daddy stayed gone more'n a month when he heard about the boys bein' killed by the Hun in some darksome forest. After that he and your mama ran away to Detroit."

Now one ray of late sun shone through the back window and struck the bottles again. The magic returned. Little bits of colored light danced around the room and threw another rainbow across Sarah's face. Aunt Wanda had the strange smell, and she sat with her hand caught between her crossed thighs just the way Daddy did. Sarah knew they were all from the same blood.

Suddenly Aunt Wanda stood up. "There's someone out there on the road. I hope it's not your Uncle Marshall Newton Stannard, come to take you back."

❧ 16 ❧

Two men ran down the hill, their words tumbling down before them. "Stop . . . blood . . . Miz Raines!" As they drew closer, Sarah heard, "Hit's the Dockery girl. She's cut bad. Hit's bleedin' her to death! Can't you come, sister?"

As they hurried up the path behind the two men, Aunt Wanda explained, "I can stop blood and blow fire," she said. "But doctors don't like it one bit, except for maybe one or two. Shoot, Dr. Spidell tried to pay me one time."

"Pay you for what?"

"Said if I'd give him the secret. Law. I declare, I wouldn't take a penny for it. I'd lose the gift, my mam said."

The Dockery house clung to the hill. Lying in the yard was a child, another towheaded child like those Sarah saw in town on Saturdays. She lay on a blanket so bloody Sarah couldn't tell what color it was. Blood dropped onto the hard dirt and little bits of dust floated atop the dark, domed circles.

Emma Jean was the girl's name. Sarah was certain that she

would have cried bloody murder if her blood had been pumping out in red spurts like a drinking fountain. But the girl did not cry; her eyes flicked back and forth to each face around her. Aunt Wanda Raines sent Sarah and a large boy scurrying up the hill. They crawled under the house as she told them to and ran back with two perfect spider's webs laid out on pieces of brown paper.

Aunt Wanda knelt down next to the girl, and Sarah saw now that she had holes in the soles of her shoes. Aunt Wanda took the webs, invisible thread by invisible thread, and laid them across the girl's wound. Blood still pumped from her leg. No one spoke as Aunt Wanda worked slowly, carefully. Then Aunt Wanda laid one big hand on the girl's leg. She put the other hand on Emma Jean's forehead.

"Quiet down, y'all. I got to think now about this child and the Lord." She bowed her head, and one or two of the men knelt down and took off their big-brimmed hats. Sarah didn't know what to do. She moved to the back of the crowd of people encircling Emma Jean.

"And when I passed by thee, Emma Jean, and saw thee polluted in thine own blood, Emma Jean, I said unto thee, Emma Jean, when thou wast in thy blood, 'Live!' Yea, I said unto thee, Emma Jean, when thou wast in thy blood, 'Live!'"

Aunt Wanda repeated the same singsongy words three times and when she finished, the child sat up. When everybody looked, the blood had stopped.

The fire had gone out in the cookstove when they came back to Aunt Wanda's. It was still hot inside so they sat on the swing, listening to the swing squeak as they pushed themselves back and forth to get cool.

"How'd you . . . make it stop like that?" Sarah asked.

"Oh, law, honey, I don't reckon I know. I don't know the wondrous way the Lord works through me. All I know— when you know the secret from Ezekiel and you say out the words and you call the person by name, bleedin' stops. And you know what else? If you never seen your own pappy, you can draw fire, you can take heat out of a burn by the very same fashion. But not you, ye'll never do it, Sarah, for you saw John Andrew."

Sarah thought that Mama's new baby would be able to draw fire and stop blood because it would never see its father, never in this world.

"Who showed you?" she asked.

"My mama. The first Sarah. And her mammy before her and her mammy before that, I reckon. It's way up past dark. Reckon we'd better be gettin' in?" Aunt Wanda tapped ashes from her pipe against the only bare place on the porch rail. The embers fell to the ground in a glowing arc. Inside, Aunt Wanda lit two coal-oil lamps. The deep goldy-glow of lamplight flickered over newspaper covered walls, and Sarah wondered if her Daddy had lain in bed reading great, dark headlines about the war to end all wars and the Armistice in 1918. Somehow she felt closer to him here than she did in town.

"If you've a mind to, look in the Bible," Aunt Wanda Raines said from the corner of the house where she pumped water to wash dishes. "It came to this county from over in Virginny. Rode on the back of a horse back in seventeen and ninety-one. Yessir, and your great-great-grandsir had a lot more books than that. One time they had to burn some. Had to keep warm, I reckon. Some of his books is gone to ash, but not the Bible. Nosir!"

Aunt Wanda was quiet for a moment and then she said, "That was the winter I was born and my pap and my only sister died and I never got to see either one. It was just me and the boys and our ma then."

How would you choose which books to burn if you were freezing, Sarah wondered. Would you close your eyes and grab up a bunch and throw them in the fireplace? She pictured pages fluttering, withering, turning to ash, all the words disappearing into the air. She remembered burning the crib and workbench back in Detroit.

"Did my father read those books?"

"Eh, law', no, honey." Aunt Wanda clattered another yellow dish into the dishpan. "He wasn't much hand to read. Said he couldn't make sense of them little squiggles, as he put it, goin' ever' which-away. Oh, he passed school, don't ye know, but he was always poundin' away at something else, 'specially after the boys died. And then he married your mama . . . you know the rest of the tale."

Sarah picked up the Bible, almost as thick as it was tall. It had a leather cover, partly eaten away and gold printing on it. She thumbed through its thin pages and found, between the Old and New Testaments, handwritten names telling the story of the Raines family. First, there was Nathaniel Raines, born in Scotland, a weaver by trade; then his sons and their sons were listed. On the bottom of the page was her father's name: John Andrew Raines, born June 20, 1894, died by his own hand March 10, 1933. *By his own hand.* There it was in black and white. Tears came to Sarah's eyes, but they were not the thick, hard tears of fear and longing. They were simpler somehow—clear, plain tears of sadness. Sarah's name was there with Mama's and the date of Mama's wedding in Detroit.

"There's going to be another name to put in here," Sarah said. "My mother is going to have another one. A baby. Soon."

She didn't know whether Mama would like it if she told Aunt Wanda, but it was almost as if she had given herself a rich and powerful gift by telling. Aunt Wanda hung a bunch of herbs from a rafter to dry and said she was happy to hear the news. Sarah wished Mama were pleased about it.

She wanted to ask Aunt Wanda more about her daddy and wanted to tell her about the terrible night, but she could not find the words. Aunt Wanda found them for her.

"I knew another man one time did what your father did. And I was there to see it all. An' try to stop the blood. That man shot his head nearly off his shoulders. Never did know why."

Aunt Wanda was so matter of fact about it, just as if she were reading a newspaper or listening to the radio. Things happened, that's all. Like a girl almost bleeding to death or a new baby coming. Sarah breathed in smoke from Aunt Wanda's pipe and felt her bigness in the room. She pictured Daddy in the loft upstairs. Aunt Wanda seemed to swell and throb and flow like a genie out of all the bottles in the room. Sarah sighed deeply, two or three times.

"Yes'm," she said.

Later, they unfolded the Murphy bed where Sarah would sleep. The bed took up every inch of space in the room and they had to step across it to wash themselves in the granite dishpan or go outside to the "little house," as Aunt Wanda called it. Sarah had never used an outhouse before. Everyone she knew had a bathroom indoors with a lock in the door. Carrying a lamp, she had to walk up a path and sit there on the wooden seat with the door open to the night. She didn't like it much. The path was wet in places, and she wondered what kind of water it might be. Her lamp cast loomy shadows on the walls and she heard an owl in a shaky *booty-hoot* nearby. On her way back to the house, she blew out her lantern and looked into the sky. She thought that the stars were ten times more beautiful than the pretend lights in the ceiling at the Riviera Theatre in Detroit. Surrounded by ghosts, uplifted by all those people in her family Bible, she thought that each real star here and now was a perfect remembrance. If only there were a star or something for Daddy, a perfect remembrance for his life, too.

Uncle Marsh picked her up before noon and when he came in to have dinner with Aunt Wanda, he acted the way he did everywhere else he went. Just as if he belonged there. In the car on the way home Sarah told him about the Bible and the moonshiner's still and mostly about Emma Jean Dockery and how Aunt Wanda Raines could stop blood.

"Well," Uncle Marsh said, "using spider's webs to stop bleeding is as old as these hills, pretty near. Your aunt is a healer, honey. And a midwife, granny woman, an herb grower, and everything else she can be to survive in these rough old mountains."

"But it can't really happen, can it?" She had seen it but couldn't quite believe what had happened right before her eyes. "Was it a trick? Shouldn't she go to the hospital?"

"Maybe it happens because they all believe it will happen.

And, no, not the hospital. They wouldn't have the money. Or the way."

When she told him about the beet leaves and Aunt Wanda's big pants moving up and down, he laughed, too. Later, Mama and Keziah told her she smelled like smoke and made her go take a bath.

🐚 17 🐚

"Say-rah! Oh, Sayrah!"

Mama's voice floated up the stairs from the hallway below, as if she were singing. She spoke in her Kentucky voice, and Sarah knew why. She wanted Sarah to come downstairs to meet Cousin Beth Ann Stannard, who had been invited to lunch. Mama was trying in the best way she knew how to tell Sarah she was sorry for the way she told about the new baby coming, sorry that everyone knew their secret about Daddy, sorry, Sarah was sure, that she was spending so much time with Aunt Wanda Raines. This was the way Mama always did things.

"I see your Mama's begun to pay attention," was the way Uncle Marsh put it when Sarah told him about the lunch.

"It is time, way past time she met someone her *own* age," was what Mama said with a sly reference to Aunt Wanda's age, conveniently forgetting that Beth Ann was seventeen years old and already going to college over in Louisville.

"Never mind. You've lived in the city. Besides—you are big for your age," Mama said when Sarah reminded her.

Now the doorbell was twisted and rang softly. When Sarah looked down through the balustrade again, Mama had her arm around Beth Ann's shoulders. Without looking, Sarah knew Beth Ann looked more like her mother than Sarah did herself. She'd seen pictures in black-paged picture albums, where, in Uncle Marsh's careful, artistic hand, he'd written her name in white ink. Staring out of pictures, Beth Ann's face was full-lipped, round, almost sleepy looking, like Mama.

There were views of Beth Ann as a baby or Beth Ann as a toddler holding Uncle Marsh's army cap and smiling at him. It was as though her cousin had stolen something from Sarah. She decided she wasn't going to like Beth Ann much.

Sarah already knew, from talking to Keziah while they put wet clothes through the wringer, that Beth Ann was her second cousin.

"She's your Grandaddy's baby brother's grandchild," Keziah said. "He was Tom Stannard and he used to keep the furniture store. He died over in Cuba when Junior wasn't but one year old. Junior is Beth Ann's daddy and your cousin Loretta is his wife."

"That would make Junior like Mama's baby. Never got to see his own father, either," Sarah said.

"Well, I don't know nothin' about that!"

"Mama's baby can blow fire and stop blood, just like—"

"Hunh! That foolishness sounds like something you carried home from Miz Wanda's. I don't know nothin' about that, either."

*   *   *

Lunch was served on the back porch. They had chicken salad and hot rolls. Keziah frosted little cakes and made iced tea served with mint in tall stemmed glasses, which soon had little beads of moisture on them. Sarah marked her initials in the cloudy film and then wiped the glass off with the corner of her skirt. She watched as the filminess formed again. Beth Ann wore a pleated skirt of white and a green blouse with a sailor collar. She and Mama matched. Mama used the sugar tongs and dabbed at her mouth with a little embroidered napkin. Sarah marveled at the way she sat up so straight. Mama was finishing things now. She was graceful again, somehow. It was as if Mama was remembering how to be, and Sarah wondered how Beth Ann had done it.

". . . don't you agree, Cousin Say-rah?"

Sarah jumped.

"I was just sayin' to your mama, Cousin Lucey?" Beth Ann talked without changing the sweet tone and quiet expression and said "cuz-zin," like that. "I was just remarkin' that we ought to go down to the Grand Dixie right quick. You know, before the picture show commences? That way, we'll get there early. You'll get to meet some of the other girls and maybe a new boy in town." She went on and on, but Sarah wasn't listening. She found herself thinking about Peter. She knew somehow that Beth Ann was the girl Peter had had to meet up on Laurel Hill.

"Thank you so much for the lovely lunch, Cousin Lucey. I am *deathly* afraid that I have made a perfect *pig* of myself over those rolls. Tell Keziah. Weren't you *darling* to invite me?" Beth Ann rushed on. Sarah understood that she expected no answer to her question. "And," she said, "Mama says y'all are to come to us real soon now that you are in town."

Sarah and Beth Ann walked up Laurel Street, past the hospital, under the arched trees over First Street toward the Grand Dixie. At Main, as they crossed in front of the Courthouse, an old man, his skin the color of ashes beneath its brownness, came toward them. He carried two heavy sacks of sugar or flour, Sarah didn't know which. She hesitated, wanted to let him pass them by with his heavy burden, but Beth Ann kept right on going. She walked right up the middle of the sidewalk, leaving the man no room at all to get past them. As they moved closer, he stepped off the sidewalk, dropped his sacks and pulled off his wide-brimmed straw hat. He stood there in the gutter, holding his hat in his hand, waiting for them to pass.

Nothing like this had ever happened to Sarah before. She didn't like it and wanted to say something to Beth Ann, but her cousin continued her monologue about dances she went to in Louisville as if nothing had happened. Sarah turned to look back at the man standing in the gutter with the Bull Durham tobacco sacks and the cigarette butts and dried up old horse apples. Why had she let him step out of their way? Why hadn't she helped him up the curbstone? Maybe that explained the sick feeling in the pit of her stomach.

"What's it like?" Beth Ann was saying.

"What's what like?" Sarah couldn't forget the man in the gutter.

"Having your father die, silly."

Sarah scuffed the toe of her new shoe against the sidewalk. "I don't know. . . ," she said.

"Did you cry?"

"No."

Beth Ann kept quiet then. As they walked along, an old chant came back to Sarah. *Step on a crack, break your father's back*. She said it over to herself as she stepped carefully on every crack in the sidewalk leading to the picture show.

❧ 18 ❧

Beth Ann paid for their tickets and talked to the cashier, who seemed to be some long-lost relative, for an everlastingly long time. Waiting there where it was hot, not stepping in under the awning, Sarah decided she hated everything about Hanlon, not just the old man with the sacks. She hated the whole place, the town with its narrow, steep streets. It was smoky and there was nothing to do; coal dust settled everywhere and she had to wash her face twice a day sometimes, especially around her nostrils. The sun went down too early behind the ever-present black mountains, pressing in on her. She wanted Nancy and Thelma and her own room and the long streetcar ride downtown to Washington Boulevard with its elegant trees.

She hated Beth Ann's cheerfulness, her easy charm with Mama. But most of all, she hated Mama and Uncle Marsh for bringing her here. Uncle Marsh brought her here, said he would care for her, and then he went off and forgot all about her. Mama was too busy sleeping and keeping whatever secret she kept, all to herself—too busy, that is, until today and the vile lunch. Sarah tried not to think about Daddy. He was the cause of it all.

She wanted to scream until her voice cracked and people stared. But she remembered her spell and couldn't do that again. She wasn't going crazy like Daddy and Aunt Wanda Raines if she could help it. One conniption fit was enough, and she didn't need Mrs. Drisdon's warning and Daddy's undershirt to do it. She wiped the perspiration off her upper lip with her hand.

"Let's sit right here," Beth Ann said. "This is where I always sit." Sarah followed her down the aisle. Beth Ann called out to two pretty girls sitting in the front row with a tall boy between them. It was Peter Daniells, bending toward one blond head and then toward the other, at ease. Sarah was surprised at the flush of pleasure and envy she felt.

"Hey! Y'all! Georgianne, Lizbeth! Peter! Come on. We're back here. I've got somebody I want you to meet."

Sarah couldn't imagine talking out loud like this in the theater at home, not with uniformed ushers and carpeted aisles and those stars glittering in the domed ceiling.

Beth Ann leaned back to whisper to Sarah. "Peter's that new boy? He's seventeen. He's going to Center College in September." She smoothed her perfect hair, just the way Mama always did. Sarah didn't mention that she already knew Peter. While the two girls and Peter moved back to sit with them, Sarah looked around. She had been in the Grand Dixie once before, with Uncle Marsh, the time they drank beer out of the same glass. She wished she could fly up into the projection booth in back and listen to the whirr of the projector instead of the sweet, musical voices of the girls. She couldn't speak to them. Her own voice would sound so flat and hard.

She yearned for the Riviera, for Nancy's familiar shape seated next to her. Where were the gold filigree cherubs and the red velvet curtain and the big theater organ? Here there was only an empty stage, a mottled screen hanging down, and a bare light bulb on a long cord swinging in front of it. Instead of warm yellow light spread on tapestried walls, there were *advertisements*. Why, Beth Ann's daddy's store name was painted here. Sarah was ashamed for her.

STANNARD HOME FURNITURE COMPANY
FURNITURE, RUGS, BEDDING
FISKER LEAF STOVES
HOOSIER KITCHEN CABINETS

Beth Ann didn't seem to notice her father's name on the walls and she spoke happily to everyone. Even though Sarah did not know who they were, except for Peter, everyone seemed to know who she was and they spoke to her as if they'd known her a long time. Of course, Peter knew so much about her that she was unable to look at him or greet him. He didn't seem to be the same quirky, almost shy boy she'd confided in.

When Georgianne and Lizbeth asked her about her mother, she realized that here she was already somebody, somebody who belonged to certain people with particular, even peculiar, ways of doing things. She was known here as a Raines, as a mountain girl, maybe a faith healer or crazy. But she was also a Stannard and all that meant about the newspaper and a big house on Laurel Street and never having to worry about money for coal and music and electricity. Here she was known "unto the generations," and it carried a terrible weight she did not want to bear. It was, she thought, as if she were a blackboard upon which many people had written all kinds of stories and messages. Was there any room for her own story? Or was she filled up with thoughts and events and actions of people she didn't even know?

". . . and this is my cousin Sarah Raines." Beth Ann was introducing the two filmy girls and Peter. "Lizbeth? Georgianne? Peter? This is Sarah Raines. She's from Detroit. It was her father who—"

The lights went out abruptly. The picture flickered onto the screen, music whined, stopped, began again, too loudly. Sarah slumped into the hard seat as thick tears filled her eyes. Now she understood that everyone knew Daddy's whole story. What was it Peter had said about living in a small town? She did not know what to do. She longed to get up and go outside, but she could not after Mama had planned it all. She stared at the screen. The picture, grainy and fluttering, was *Winds of Desolation*. Watching John Wayne and his partner as they rode into a broken down, deserted ghost town, she understood exactly how they felt. She sat through the movie, not knowing what else to do. She prayed for the end of it. When it was over, she'd hurry over to Uncle Marsh's office in the next building. She would not walk home with those pretty girls and Peter, who sat now in the seat close to Beth Ann, his eyes fixed on the screen.

The lights flashed on. Before she could edge out of her seat to run up the aisle, Beth Ann put her hand on Sarah's arm.

"Psst!" she said. "It's not over. They're having something extra this afternoon. It's Uncle Dave Macon here to sing."

Without looking at the audience, three men wandered out onto the bare stage from the wings, carrying their own chairs. The men wore clean, plain clothes instead of costumes or evening clothes. Singing in nasal tones, the way John Andrew used to sing to Sarah, they played the violin, a five string guitar, and banjo with fingers that flew over the strings so fast Sarah couldn't understand how their hands and their memories kept up with each other. Their fingers were like hummingbirds at the nectar of music. Although this was not a church, the man they called the Dixie Dewdrop, Uncle Dave, sang a hymn or two and then finally sang: ". . . though we meet with the darkness and strife, it will help us every day, it will brighten all our way, if we keep on the sunny side, always on the sunny side, keep on the sunny side of life."

19

"Uncle Dave" stepped out onto the apron of the stage when his song was over to ask if a certain Mr. Bayliss Arnett was in the audience. "And if he is," Uncle Dave said, "why doesn't he come on up here and set in with us? Pick a tune or two?"

Then, while a stocky man with a guitar slung across his back came up the aisle, Uncle Dave went on telling why Bayliss Arnett was in Hanlon.

"He's one of them college boys." He smiled. "But not like some we had up here in nineteen and thirty-one when our coal miners struck for a union. This one's from Lexington. He can sing and play guitar some. If the facts were known, he writes down some of this queer old music we play and sing here in the mountains. Then he'll go back and write up a book about it."

Bayliss Arnett told how he'd come to town from over in North Carolina. He'd listened to a lot of music over there, he said, and now he wanted to do the same thing right here.

When he picked up his guitar, he played and sang so sweetly that Sarah forgot that she wanted to run out of the picture show. When he finished, he said, "If any of y'all know anyone who writes down new songs they make up or sings the old ones, I'd be mighty grateful. . . ."

Someone in the back spoke up. "If you're a'lookin' for something in this town, the best place to go is the newspaper office. Mr. Marshall Stannard'd know where to send ye."

When she heard this, Sarah changed her mind about escaping into Uncle Marsh's office after the show was over. That young man, Mr. Arnett, would go straight over there right now with his guitar slung over his back. So, after all, she had to go have a Coca-Cola with Beth Ann and her friends. She ordered it with a squirt of ammonia in it the way Beth Ann did and she sat in the leather-covered booth sipping the cold drink, listening to the girls talk to each other. She tried to enter in the way Mama would expect, but they didn't seem to notice whether she was there or not. Peter didn't sit with them in the booth but perched on a stool up at the fountain and talked to the boy behind the counter. He lifted the straws out of his glass of orange crush and pretended to check out the state of their cleanliness. Then he waved them at Sarah and made a face as if he'd tasted something awful.

By the time Sarah got home, Mama and Uncle Marsh were there on the front porch together with nobody else in this world but Mr. Bayliss Arnett. They were all drinking Mama's newest rage, that greenish Seven-Up soda pop. When he stood up to meet her, she saw that he was only a little taller than she was, with heavy arms and shoulders as if he'd been lifting something heavy. He was younger than he seemed at first, younger than Mama and Uncle Marsh. He looked as if he'd been sitting here on their front porch every day of his life, with his legs crossed at the ankle, waving his glass like an orchestra leader's baton. He was telling Mama about wandering the hills of North Carolina in search of songs from Elizabethan times and how he got to know some of the old people up in the hills and hollows and got them to sing by singing to them first. He ran his fingers through his brown hair, which fitted his head like a cap, as he talked and never took his eyes off Mama the whole time.

Of course, Mama acted the same as she always did whenever Uncle Marsh brought somebody home. He did this as often as he could so Mama would have to put something on and help Keziah with the food. Uncle Marsh was acting just as nice as you please, too, and not saying anything to rile Mama about the government projects and the President. Bayliss called him FDR as though he knew him and liked him, but Mama said she couldn't approve of all the programs that the Democrats thought up to ruin the country. She and Uncle Marsh argued about politics nearly every night until they went indoors to sing and play the piano after it got dark. Now Mama wasn't arguing but listening carefully with her head tilted, a slight flush to her cheeks. The light fell on her deeply veed organdy collar, Grandmama's pearls at her throat.

"It is about suppertime, Mr. Arnett. Why don't we ask Keziah to set another place for you?"

There was a flutter inside the house as Keziah moved away from her place at the screen door with its curliques and knobs and elaborate decoration. Sarah went inside to help.

After dinner they came into the living room and talked about the Depression, hard times again. It was all anyone ever talked about, Sarah thought.

"They're saying sixteen million people are out of a job now," Mr. Arnett said as Uncle Marsh lit his cigarette from the lighted end of his own.

"Read recently, somewhere or other"—Uncle Marsh breathed smoke out of his nostrils—"that more people left the U.S. than came into the country. People went back to Europe to find work."

"That's a first, isn't it?" Mr. Arnett said.

"All I know—there's no work for miners here. You'd never know it but we had a boom year five years ago. No one buys coal now and miners are starving, they say, though they won't talk about it."

Sarah wanted to say Aunt Wanda wasn't starving, but she knew she was supposed to be seen and not heard. She sat on the metal window seat covering the radiator and watched Mr. Arnett and Mama and Uncle Marsh.

Mama sat in a chair near the floor lamp with the fringed shade so that her figure was silhouetted against the back wall. She looked to Sarah like one of the paper cutouts of children's profiles they did at Hudson's Department Store in Detroit. Uncle Marsh said, "You read about the coal operators giving the miners a ten-cent raise? In four states they did that." But Mr. Arnett wasn't listening to one word Uncle Marsh said. He was staring at Mama as if he'd never seen anything like her before.

"Your brother tells me, Mrs. Raines, that you are a musician, have a fine musical voice? You've studied?" Mr. Arnett crossed his legs as he stretched them out in front of him.

"Well," Mama said, "yes, but . . . oh, that was a long time ago. And at an insignificant girl's school."

Mama turned her body in the straight comb-backed chair, away from Mr. Arnett's gaze.

"Lucey is not telling you the whole story," Uncle Marsh said. "Lucey had a mighty fine teacher, French he was."

"Professor Asnogarde?" Mama smiled. "Yes, from Paris. Paris, France. Papa always wanted me to go there to study. But the war and. . . ." Mama's voice trailed away like a line of ink on a paper. Sarah knew she was thinking about Daddy and living in Detroit and being poor.

"Lucey, why don't we sing some with Mr. Arnett tonight? We sing nearly every night, Mr. Arnett. You know, 'My Old Kentucky Home,' songs like that?"

Uncle Marsh played the notes and Mr. Arnett stood behind him and they sang. Mama still sat across the room, not joining in, though Sarah knew she wanted to. The comb-backed chair formed a fan around the back of her head. Sarah heard her hum and whisper the soft words.

"Mama, it's so much better when you sing. Come on."

Mama complained about her lack of practice, said she'd forgotten all she ever knew, but Sarah knew that was not so. Mama practiced, or used to, for hours at a time sometimes. *Mah-mah, mee-mee, may-may, moh-moh, moo-moo . . . may, mee, moh, moo.* So with their eyes and by nodding their heads at Mama and then at the music, they insisted she join in.

"The sun shines bright on my old Kentucky home . . . ," Mama began, softly as before, growing stronger and more vibrant with each phrase.

"Ain't no bird prettier," Uncle Marsh said above a pause in the music. Mama sang and Mr. Arnett sang, too, the two clear sounds twining together as true as air. They were like vines, Sarah thought, or like bodies, but she didn't know where that thought came from. Maybe it was something she'd seen in the art museum back home in Detroit.

Mama went to get some iced tea for everybody because Keziah had gone to prayer meeting and only had time to lay out date-filled cookies she and Sarah made the day before. Sarah could hardly wait to tell Keziah about Mama's singing. Mama's face was flushed and she had a golden glow to replace the sallow, dry-eyed look she'd had for so long. She moved about the room, passing cookies around, bending at the waist, tilting her head in her unique way, and smiling into Mr. Arnett's eyes. Mr. Arnett stared and stared at her, lingering over everything Mama said, watching her pearls sway against her body.

While they drank their tea, Uncle Marsh pretended he was Rudy Vallee on the Fleischman Radio Hour and sang to them in a hollow voice like his. They laughed at him and then Mama and Uncle Marsh danced around the room, stirring up the Persian rug and loosening the hair on Mama's neck. Still breathless from swirling and turning, Marsh took Mama's hand in his and looked deep into her eyes. Sarah thought then that they looked exactly like Nelson Eddy and Jeannette MacDonald, and Uncle Marsh's scar hardly showed at all. She yearned to have him look at her, hold her, and dance with her like that.

". . . Lucey," he was saying, "I want you to sing one more . . . ." He moved to the piano and pulled a new sheaf of music from the piano bench. Mama leaned over his shoulder to see the notes on the page, rippling and strung together like Christmas lights. Uncle Marsh played the first chords.

"Ah! *Rigoletto!*" Mr. Arnett sighed and sat down.

"Marsh, no, I can't." Mama twisted her hands together.

"Oh, honey, sure you can. 'Caro Nome.' We're not the Metropolitan. You can do it for us. Just for us."

Sarah could tell her mother half wanted to sing it and half did not. And not because it was hard or anything. It was because she used to sing it for Daddy. But Mama cleared her throat and put one hand in the other, palms up, as though she were holding the notes. She stood erect and breathed deeply. Sarah did not dare to look at Mr. Arnett.

> *"Caro no-me che-il mio cor.*
> *Fes-ti pri-mo pal-pi-tar.*
> *Dear name within this breast*
> *Thy memory will remain."*

Mama's voice was so full of longing that Sarah wanted to cry. She also wanted to sing, to let her voice join Mama's, to let the feelings soar, but her throat was too full and she did not know the melody. She lay back on the cushions, awash in the sound of Mama's voice.

"Car-o no-me che-il mi-o cor!"

Sarah saw Mama's face crumple like paper before her voice broke. She ran upstairs and the two men stood looking after her. To Sarah it seemed that Mama was one half of a photograph and Uncle Marsh and Mr. Arnett were the other half, thrown onto the floor.

❧ 20 ❧

"It's time. If the truth were known, it's way past time. We've been here a decent interval. Sarah ought to have a real party, meet some young people. Not, you know, not a cotillion. Not one of those grand dances, nothing like that. But something nice, really nice."

Mama was talking to Bay Arnett. Everyone called him Bay now, and he'd been coming up to the house nearly every day since that first time when Mama sang for him. Mornings they went out in Bay's car, out into the countryside looking for people to sing their old songs for him so he could write the music down in his notebooks. Mama's name and her presence helped people accept him, and she encouraged the old people to sing for him. When he found a new song or new words to old tunes, Sarah typed them out on Uncle Marsh's boxy Underwood in his room next to the porch. Over the clack, clack, clack of the keys Sarah listened to Mama and Bay talk about her. Sometimes they gossiped about Uncle Marsh and Miss Bennet and how he was never going to marry her, not in this world, he wasn't. Sarah wanted Mama to be right about that. She took a clean piece of paper and typed onto its whiteness, "It is not unlawful to marry your uncle." Nancy told her it was when Sarah wrote that she was going to ask him to marry her some day. She folded the paper into a tiny square, and hesitating only a moment, she put it in her uncle's top desk drawer.

"I've paid no attention to her, poor child," Mama was saying. "I know it. Nobody has to tell me. But there have been so many . . . things to get used to. I—I want to make it up to her. All those things that have happened."

"You can't, Lucey," Bay said. "You can't make up for it. No matter how hard you run."

"Well, I want her to have something to do. Writing letters back home? Reading Book-of-the-Month Club books? She's ruining her eyes. Besides, I'm not sure those are the books for her. *The Good Earth?* I haven't even read it. Isn't it too old?"

"But why a party?" Bay said. "She's doing fine the way she is. Besides, she's in there typing out those songs for me. I don't want you to keep her too busy for that."

"You know," Mama said, acting as if she hadn't heard one word Bay said, "she takes after the Raineses. She gets so inside herself. Can't talk to anybody. Well, they were hill people for generations back, hidden in the hollows—no wonder."

The chains of the swing squealed and Sarah wanted to get up and look out the window to see if they were sitting closer together. It was getting to be like a movie, where the stars sit on the swing together and hold hands. Sarah didn't see how Mama could act as if she were some movie star in love.

Didn't Mama remember that she was already married and more than that, she was going to have a baby? Something about Mama's voice when she talked to Bay, something musical in it that made you think she wanted him to know something she couldn't say out loud, made Sarah feel twitchy, and she didn't like it one bit.

". . . leave her be," Bay said again. "She doesn't need a party. She needs time. It's hard to lose your father. She's got a lot to. . . ."

"Well, all right. All I know is if it were me, I'd want to meet some boys and—"

Bay said something under his breath that Sarah couldn't hear. But she did hear Mama gasp and then laugh. She put the cover on the typewriter and went out of the room. She didn't want to hear, or not hear, any more of Mama's talk with Bay.

It didn't matter, finally, what Bay or anyone else said. When Mama made up her mind to give a party, it stayed made up. They gave the party. It was all part of her plan to be a better mother to Sarah, to prove something to herself. For two days, she wore a dust cap over her long hair as she and Keziah cleaned and dusted and scoured every inch of the house. James, Keziah's son, came to mow lawns and trim front hedges, and Sarah swept walks and wiped off thirteen pieces of green wicker furniture on all three porches. Counting each piece as she knelt on the gray wood floor, she wished she were somewhere else, doing something else. She didn't want a party, but when Mama asked her, she said yes because she didn't want to make her sad again. Mrs. Drisdon came to her mind for the first time in a long time.

Keziah baked cookies and iced some of those little cakes and Uncle Marsh stayed down at Miss Bennet's as much as he could. When he wasn't down at her house, Amanda Bennet, her skirts fluttering, came winding up the hill to see how things were going. Sarah was sure she didn't wear one single thing beneath those silky dresses, and she didn't want her in the sewing room while Mama fitted her party dress. She didn't want her there to tell Mama how to tame Sarah's hair with green hair-setting lotion from the five-and-dime either, but she was.

The party was scheduled to begin at eight, after it was dark enough for the colored lights to show, Mama decided. And it turned out to be a hot, damp Saturday night. Because Mama made her, before the guests arrived, Sarah collected all the items for the Identify game.

"It'll get everyone acquainted and break the ice," Mama said. "Go on now. Don't sulk. It spoils your looks. I declare, one of these days, your face is going to freeze that way. Just get twenty-five little things. You know, a button, a piece of coal—oh, a spoon. Ask Keziah for a dime. Lay them out on the tray."

After the tray was filled, she said, "See? You pass paper and pencils to everyone. Then they'll have one minute to look, to memorize it all. And the one who remembers the most wins. Sarah, you can't play because you already know all the things, don't you? That would be cheating—oh, not cheating exactly, just not fair. Instead you can practice memorizing everyone's name and being sweet."

Sarah already felt separate, set aside from the others. She was too thin, too wild-haired and she didn't know how to talk smoothly to Beth Ann and Georgianne and Lizbeth, who came in together. They stood in the front hall with Mama, their voices rising and falling like poles on a musical calliope, all separate and yet together in a preordained pattern. Where they were pink and gold, Sarah felt dark, olive-skinned; where they were graceful, Sarah felt awkward and looked down at her feet to make certain she hadn't worn Mrs. Drisdon's old blue shoes by mistake. Where they could talk on and on about nothing as if it were everything, Sarah could say nothing at all. She arranged and rearranged the pieces on the tray. Her fingers were blackened by the lump of coal she moved like a chess piece from place to place. She rubbed her hands down the side of her new pink dress before she remembered she was all dressed up.

The next to arrive were the two little boys from across the street, who were too young to be there at all, but Mama had said, "Mrs. Glancy'll be offended if she looks over here and sees all the colored lanterns lit up and hears a party goin' on and her boys not invited." So, here they were, their hair slicked down and their fingernails scraped. Wearing long pants, they came in and stood behind the fern in the hall and snapped paper wads at each other and sometimes at the older boys and girls.

Peter Daniells came up the front walk with three more tall, thin boys. Mama whispered, "Peter's daddy was my first real beau, you know. We were engaged to be married one time. Did I tell you that?" She tilted her head and went forward, smiling, to greet the young men.

"Well, now that you are all here"—Mama clapped her hands and everybody gathered round—"we're goin' to play Identify. Sarah will pass out among you. . . ." Mama put her hand over her mouth and shrugged up her shoulders and laughed. No one else did. *Why does Mama have to try to be funny? Does she think she's one of the young people?*

"Sarah, honey, you take the pencils and paper around. Y'all have just one minute to look at the tray and memorize everything."

When everyone was busy concentrating on the trayful of things, Mama stood close to Sarah. "Sam Daniells, Peter's father? He was the most *peculiar* thing. When he'd dance with you he'd put a double-damask linen table napkin between your bare back and his bare hand. I believe to my soul he carried one with him for just that purpose. It was . . . ," Mama looked for just the right word, "insulting. Right insulting."

One of the little boys broke his pencil and Mama went to get him another. She made everybody wait and not play until she got back.

"After that I just didn't want him comin' back up here to see me anymore. That's when I began to ride out to Papa's mine with him and I saw Johnnie . . . your daddy." She looked out of the window at the lights blinking in the trees. "Now, of course," she said and smoothed her skirt, "Sam Daniells is a fine doctor practicing up in Cincinnati."

Peter lounged against the fireplace with his arms folded across his chest. The lamp shone into his eyes, making him look owlish and blank, but Sarah remembered his green eyes, green as Uncle Marsh's behind the glasses. He put his pencil behind his ear and watched everyone struggle to remember. It was obvious to Sarah he didn't want to play this childish game any more than she did. He was just too polite to refuse. Everyone was too polite to refuse. Mama went on. "He spends summers here in Hanlon. Has for years. His mother . . . she can't take care of him. Keziah says she's in the asylum for the insane. She had a . . . she lost a child. Drove her out of her mind."

So that was Peter's secret. How easily Mama told it, and with no malice aforethought. Peter's secret was that his mother really was crazy, crazy enough to be put away. Sarah looked at him, trying to imagine how he might feel. She could imagine. She had the same feelings.

Now Mama floated around the room, telling everyone they could *so* remember, encouraging them, giving broad hints: "It'll burn in a stove" or "Put one on your shirt to close it." She laughed up at the tall boys as if her very life depended on everyone playing Identify with her. *No*, Sarah thought, *it is as if this is her party. She's the one who needs it.*

Beth Ann closed her eyes and put her hands over her ears so she wouldn't hear Mama's hints, and she tipped her head back so she'd have been looking at the ceiling with the plaster rosette in the center if her eyes had been open. Sarah could almost see her thinking, picturing before she wrote anything down. She won the prize Sarah wanted for herself, the bottle of Cutex "Pink Rapture" nail polish and the box of body powder decorated with a design like fireworks or feathers.

Now it was time for the Five-Minute Date game Mama invented, the one that Bay and Uncle Marsh laughed so hard about. It was Mama's idea to have these little dates: Each boy would have a chance to meet each girl so there would be no pairing off, leaving someone out, Mama said, looking hard at Sarah.

"Everyone will get to know everyone else. Let's not have those awful kissing games. No Spin the Bottle or Post Office tonight," she said, as if she didn't mean one word of it.

123

Now she clapped her hands again and everyone encircled her as if she were the maypole and they were dancers with ribbons in their hands. Sarah had a vision of Mama's body wrapped in colored ribbons, around and around until she couldn't move, like the Egyptian mummy at the art museum.

"Each girl has a little card," Mama said. "Listen now, y'all. You boys must sign every girl's card at least one time. Then you'll have five minutes to do whatever you want. You could walk around the yard. You could come in the house and play records on the Victrola, swing in the yard swing. Little dates, you see?"

She was going to make everyone have a good time or know the reason why, but Sarah had to admit that everyone seemed to like Mama's idea. There was a great hubbub as cards were signed and returned and erased and signed again. Trades were made. Sarah tried not to look at Peter, didn't want to know whose card he signed first. It was not hers. The two little boys from across the street fought over Sarah's card until she took it away from them. When she finally handed it to Peter it was smudged and crumpled.

By the time Mama rang her little bell to begin the first date, Sarah's first date had gone home to bed, so she spent the time on the front porch with Keziah before Keziah went down the street to church. They watched everyone disappear down the back hill or around the side of the house. Peter and Beth Ann wandered into the tall hedge across the side yard and Sarah made herself look away from their close dark figures in the shadows.

Sarah's next date was with one of the tall, skinny boys who had come in with Peter. He wanted to stay in the dining room to drink lemonade, eat Keziah's date-filled cookies, and listen to Uncle Marsh's Sir Harry Lauder records. He liked winding the handle of the Victrola too tightly so voices came out speeded up. When the five minutes were up Sarah was happy to hear Mama's little bell ring. The boy hadn't said anything to her at all. Next on Sarah's card was Jay, the oldest of the two little Glancy boys across the street. He took her arm as Mama suggested and led her down Miss Bennet's hill, down the little winding stone walk covered with moss and shining with water that trickled down from Laurel Hill above. At Miss Bennet's gate he showed her his Tom Mix Decoder Badge.

"I'm a real Ralston Straight Shooter," he whispered and pulled a little pistol out of his pocket. "Listen, I've got a real good secret you ought to know. It'll cost you ten cents to see it and it's worth every penny."

When she would not pay he led her into the lilac bushes behind Miss Bennet's house anyway.

"Look up," he whispered, and Sarah thought he looked like a snake, with his hair slicked back, his little narrow face and his tongue flicking back and forth across tiny teeth. "Go on, look in that window there."

She didn't know what made her follow his lead, take orders from him, but she pushed her way through the dense hedge close against the house as little twigs pulled at her hair and dead, brown lilac blossoms stuck to her sweaty skin. She held onto the windowsill and pulled herself up on the drain pipe. She steadied herself against the house and looked into the window.

Uncle Marsh and Miss Bennet were in bed together. Sarah ducked her head so she wouldn't have to look again, but not before Uncle Marsh stood up. He was "stark naked" as

Daddy put it, and she saw the curve of his buttocks and long, thin legs. She saw, too, Miss Bennett's golden, naked shoulders and laughing face as she pointed at the window where Sarah clung. Something she'd never felt before moved in Sarah's body. She closed her eyes, let herself slip to the ground. Jay Glancy sang under his breath, "Sally Rand has lost her fan. Give it back, you nasty man."

She wanted to die. Why was Uncle Marsh there with Miss Bennet like that? She knew now. He was always there—even the first night when he'd caught her flinging the blossom into the oak tree. How could he? She, Sarah, was the only one he loved. She knew it was true. Even if he hadn't said so. Sarah knew he didn't need anyone else. Not even Mama. Hadn't he been the one to talk to her when she grieved for her father? Hadn't he found Aunt Wanda Raines for her, helped her find the other part of herself? She was his. No one could come between. Still crouching beneath the window in the lilacs, she fought back a scream or vomit.

Now, she thought, they'll have to get married and what will become of me then? And Mama? How could they stay there with Miss Bennet in Grandmama's house? All the knots inside that had seemed to float away tied themselves up again. She wanted to strike out at something. She turned to run, to find the snake-eyed little boy, to hit him. She hated him for telling her, for showing her his dirty little Ralston Straight Shooter secret, the mean child not old enough to know what he had done. She wanted to slap him, slap his snake-eyed face, but he was gone. She ran, scrabbling back up the hill. She heard a door slam inside Miss Bennet's house, heard Mama's little bell ring. Mama was giving it an extra shake just for her.

She wanted to get away from the rest of the silly little dates, from the colored lights in the trees where James had strung them, and away from all the young people milling around Mama laughing and talking all at once. She could not go up there and face them now.

But then she remembered. Her next date was with Sam Daniell's son, Peter. She felt perspiration slide down the side of her body, staining the new dress Mama made her and wetting the lace around the little capelike sleeves. Her hair had escaped the pasting down Mama and Miss Bennet had given it and jangled around her face. No lightning bugs flickered in the light given off by colored paper lanterns hanging in the trees. Sarah supposed they were frightened of the varicolored lights and might be meeting somewhere high up in the oaks to decide what to do about the interlopers. She thought about the lightning bugs, their yellow-green glow and cobwebbed wings, so she wouldn't have to think about Uncle Marsh and how he had betrayed her.

❧ 21 ❧

"What do you want to do?" It was Peter claiming his date
with her.

Mama looked relieved, hot, and frazzled. Her hair had escaped the neat knot on the back of her head and her face was
red. She pushed a strand of Sarah's hair back behind one ear
and smiled at Peter—hopefully, Sarah thought.

"What do you want to do?" Peter repeated.

"I don't care, what do you?"

"Nothing, I guess." They walked arm in arm the way
Mama had told them all to do. At least they walked that way
until Mama went indoors.

"You like this stuff?" he asked, letting his arm hang down
his side, leaving her holding onto his limp arm, as if it were a
rope.

She didn't want him to feel sorry for her. She straightened
the hem of her dress.

"Not me," she said. "Do you?"

"Well, I can see your mama is having a fine time. I reckon everybody is."

"I'm going downtown," Sarah said.

"Now? We have only five minutes," he said, but she knew they were going to walk downtown anyway and maybe never even come back. That's what she wanted to do. Never come back and have to look at Uncle Marsh again. She had a strange, mysterious feeling in her then and wanted to run and shout and tear her hair and pound something. They walked. The warm glow of streetlights flickered through dark green leaves overhead. Instead of taking Peter's hand and running very fast, maybe even flying away from there, she walked with one foot on the curbstone and one foot in the street in a gimpy way, making a rhythmic, off-beat sound in the summer street. The noise of the party faded as if a radio program had been turned down. They did not speak as they walked past the school where Miss Bennet taught English composition and Manifest Destiny, and Sarah tried not to think about her golden shoulders, her hair. They didn't speak until they passed the hospital where the Auston boy died last week. "His mother had to sit there and watch him die," Sarah told Peter and he nodded. They kept on walking and Sarah felt that she had never felt so close to anyone in her whole life before. Not even Nancy. Did he feel it too, behind his thick glasses?

They came to the place where Keziah's people lived. Here there were no streetlights and the street was unpaved. Sarah knew this place. She had walked home with Keziah sometimes to visit Aunt Sude or brought Uncle Marsh's shirts down to Keziah's oldest girl to do up. But that was always in broad daylight. She'd never been here at night. She heard the tinny sound of a bluesy song played on someone's radio. A dog barked as they walked by a fenced-in yard. Peter picked up a stick and dragged it across a fence. When it clackety-clacked in the dark someone yelled, "G'wan! Git!"

They came to a wooden bridge arched across the river. Beneath them, on the riverbank below, was the Holiness Church where Keziah and most of her friends went almost every day at least once. Music from the church piano floated up from below them as they stood on the bridge. The river ran, shining like a black satin ribbon from the ten-cent store, silently in the darkness. Sarah remembered the streetcar tracks back home in Detroit, how they gleamed in the dark, too, and the yellow streetcars filled with men going to the factories in the early morning before it was light.

The doors to the church were open and people inside sat on folding chairs, fanning themselves. The women wore white dresses and flowered hats. The pounding of the music and the yellow light made Sarah feel fine. She felt warm and tense, not relaxed and soft, but tense as if something were going to happen and she did not know what it would be. She clasped her hands behind her head and leaned back against the bridge rail. She felt as though she and Peter were waiting in the wings of a giant stage, waiting to go on and say their piece and act out their part in the play. It was just that she didn't know her part.

"Come on. Let's go," Peter said.

"Nope. I'm staying here. I like it here. Don't you?"

"Come on."

"You go on. Go back if you want to. I'm staying." She felt

a deep stubbornness in her grow and flow through her body and make a hard place in her brain.

"You've got no business here."

She didn't even know this boy, she thought, and here he was telling her what she didn't want to hear. She tried to cover up her ears, but he took her hands and pulled her back up the hill, back across the bridge.

"Come on now," he said. "Enough is enough. Don't be a dope." He walked backward, drawing her with him. He seemed embarrassed, afraid, stubborn as she. She felt as if they were puppets performing on the bridge with its low, curved arch over the river.

She pulled away from Peter. He started across the bridge toward town. Stopping at the top of the hill, he turned to wait for her to catch up, but she would not; she couldn't go back. There on the bridge under the streetlight, she couldn't think of anything to say. She could only wish that he would stay there with her. He put his hands in his pockets and kicked at something—a stone, maybe. Then suddenly, as if he saw something he hadn't seen before, he ran back toward her. He grabbed her hand and they headed for the hard-packed dirt path, laughing like two crazy people. There was a thicket of wild roses along either side of the clay bank, still slippery from a summer rain. Her long dress caught in the brambles and, held fast, she stumbled. She waited while he loosed her dress from the thorns, holding on to the curved branch of a fallen willow tree with one hand. Then they hurried down the riverbank to the front door of the church.

Of course, Keziah was there. Sarah pointed her out to Peter. Towering over the rest, she was unmistakable. She wore a cream-colored straw hat with a wide, curved brim and three peach silk peonies, their thin petals curled at the edges, and tiny yellow silk balls gathered at the center. Sarah stared at the wonderful hat and wondered where Keziah got it. She knew that Keziah looked the best of any of the ladies.

The preacher, Mr. Caldwell, who was by day the owner of a grocery store, stood now on a raised platform in the center of the room. He wore brown pants and a blue coat with a narrow red stripe in it, a white shirt and a black bow tie. Sarah sat down on a bench with Peter.

". . . I have a few announcements. There'll be dinner on the ground next Sunday a week," Mr. Caldwell said in his rich, deep preacher-voice. "My Lord!" he said, "Sister Jessie here says the choir will provide the corn bread. I say the Lord . . ."

"All right!"

". . . will provide. And Jesus took the fishes and lo! he fed the multitudes."

"Amen!"

". . . it's the Devil wants you to be poor and broke."

"That's the truth!" someone in the congregation said.

"We are going to shake the Devil up. The hell with the Devil!"

Everybody laughed and clapped at that remark. Peter laughed too and leaned forward, holding the edge of the bench with both hands.

A man waved his cane and said, "The hell with the Devil is right, preacher man." And someone, Sarah couldn't see who it was, said, "And the hell with the Depression, too." No one ever talked like this at the Methodist Church where Sarah had gone a few times with Uncle Marsh. They always sat in church in a dignified and separate silence as Reverend Mr. Simpson spoke as if to strangers.

"Well, God is a way-maker, that's for certain sure," Mr. Caldwell said.

"*My Lord!*" The congregation answered him. Everything in the room, Sarah thought, seemed to throb, to pulsate like a heart beating. Someone began to clap his hands. Sarah wanted to join in but she couldn't let herself. She looked over at Peter. He tapped his feet and, still leaning forward, elbows on knees, he looked over his shoulder at her, grinning with the pleasure of it.

"No man can save a soul!" Mr. Caldwell shouted. "The Lord said, 'Behold I make all things new!'"

"*Amen!*"

"Have a mind to serve the Lord! Now!"

Someone rattled a tambourine. Sally Kate Crawford, a friend of Keziah's, played some chords on the piano. Sarah felt the rhythm of the music ripple across the room and the beat of Mr. Caldwell's words throbbed in the soles of her feet and in the back of her neck. The piano got louder and louder. Mr. Caldwell turned around to look at Sally Kate.

"Now, girl, don't trouble my mind here with the music yet. When the Lord is workin' his spirit through my body, He don't take to no foolishness."

Sally Kate put her hands in her lap, but she smiled and tapped her foot at the same time.

"My Father's house has many mansions. If it were not so I would have told you." Mr. Caldwell's voice rose again and he began to build up the tempo of his preaching.

"I am going to read from the twenty-eighth chapter of Deuteronomy."

"All right!"

"And it shall come to pass if thou shalt harken diligently unto the voice of the Lord, to do all his commandments, the Lord thy God will set thee on high above all nations of the earth. The Lord shall make thee the head. And thou shalt be above only!"

The preacher's voice rose, the veins in his neck bulged out in knots, and Sarah thought if they burst, she would be spattered with his blood. Keziah, tall and beautiful, dabbed at her face with a handkerchief. Sarah felt as if her heart would burst with pride and love for Keziah and with something else she could not name. Then someone in the back started a song and the clapping took up when the preacher stopped long enough to wipe his glistening face with a handkerchief and drink a dipperful of cold water from a bucket.

"Daniel in the li-on's den!" they sang.

Then a frenzy of action started, arm waving, hand clapping, foot stomping. Sarah felt the bang, bang, banging of the rhythm. She thought she was surely possessed by the glory of the Lord. She could stand it no longer. She stood up and raised her arms over her head and shouted out with the others, "Daniel in the lion's den!"

Her hands stung with the clapping together. No one seemed to pay any attention to her and Peter at all until Sarah pushed her way out into the aisle and marched around the room with the others. She lost sight of Peter but she sang, sang for happiness.

Then Keziah saw her. Heard her, maybe. She reached out one big hand to drag her into the chair beside hers. Peter, who marched around the crowded, steamy, hot room, marched right out the front door. He left her there with Keziah and went out into the darkness.

❧ 22 ❧

Already taller than anyone else, anyhow, when she pulled herself up to the fullness of her anger, Keziah was an awesome sight to see. She held Sarah's arm up at an awkward angle with her cool, dry, long fingers and propelled her through the crowd without speaking to a soul. Sarah wanted to smile and nod to everyone she knew, but no one looked at her. Sarah tried to decide about the look on Keziah's face. How angry was she? Keziah'd been disgusted with Sarah before. Just last week, Sarah had taken the last slice of peach pie or tracked in on Keziah's clean floor, she couldn't remember which, and Keziah had pushed her out of the kitchen. But this look was different. There was no fondness or forgiveness behind the words. Sarah wouldn't be wrapped in Keziah's arms afterward and hugged to her spicy, fragrant breast, forgiven.

Sarah felt anger flow from Keziah's crackly hand through her arm like electric current.

"Who you think you are?" was what Keziah said finally.

"Who in this world you think you are?" She said it again and didn't wait for an answer, although Sarah did not know what she would have answered to the question. Didn't Keziah know who she was? Just herself? But Keziah went on and on about how Sarah came into her own church, her own *sanctuary*, to shame her. She said she didn't have anything in this world she could call her own, and now Sarah came there and robbed her of even that beggarly mite. Sarah didn't understand half of what Keziah was talking about in that weary tone of voice with scarcely enough strength, it seemed, to speak.

"One of these days," she said at last, "one of these days . . . I'm goin' snatch ever' one of y'all baldheaded." It seemed funny and mean to Sarah at the same time, but Keziah did not mean it be be funny, she knew that for certain.

It was dark and Keziah was swallowed up in shadow. Only her light dress and her eyes were shining. She had taken off the marvelous hat and held it down at her side like a dead bouquet. Sarah was sure it was something else Keziah was angry at, like Mama's anger when Daddy came home sick drunk sometimes. Mama would yell at Sarah then instead of Daddy, and this was what Keziah was doing right now, Sarah thought. Keziah's fury was simply not about some little old white girl parading around her church clapping her hands and shouting.

"I don't see why you're so mad. Mama's been to your church. She told me. Lots of—"

Keziah let go of Sarah's arm with push enough to make Sarah stumble, her feet making scrabbling noises on loose gravel. The sound seemed more real than Keziah and her anger.

"She was invited!" Keziah spat out the words. "You had no call to come down here pokin' your nose in. Makin' fun of us poor folks! How come you to leave your nice party? Didn't you want to bring every one of those fine people down here to the Bottoms?"

"No! Cross my heart and hope to die." Sarah wanted to say she was sorry, but she was not. She wasn't sorry about being in the Holiness Church with Peter and singing with everybody, rejoicing about something all together, the way Mr. Caldwell said. Keziah took it all wrong.

"Git. G'wan. Git!" Keziah said. "Outta my sight."

And then, in his shirt sleeves, smoking a cigarette, Uncle Marsh appeared out of the darkness and Sarah had to face the rest of her night. She had to think about Peter's leaving her and about Uncle Marsh and Miss Bennet. She had to think about running away from Mama's party and all the guests and the five-minute dates.

She couldn't bear to look at him, seeing him now dressed in all his clothes, smoking, walking around just as though nothing had happened. She couldn't let him look at her, either, because if he did, he would know what she had seen. But when he came toward her out of the shadows and put his arm around her shoulders, she let him once more and wondered why.

"Sarah, honey, your Mama's mighty indignant right now. Got anything to say for yourself?"

"No, sir."

"What made you leave?"

"Had a five-minute date with Peter. . . . Oh, why did you have to be there with her . . . ," she cried out before she knew what she would say.

"Damn! So that's it. You were the one in the bushes! Sarah, what a thing to do! What did you expect, peekin' around in the dark?"

"I thought you loved me. You were nice to me and took me places and talked to me about my daddy. I thought you loved *me!*"

She put her hands over her face and felt the cold tears wet her cheeks.

"Sarah, I do love you. But not . . . not that way. I love you because you are a child. Because you look like me. Because you are my blood and we have the same history. But not as if you were a woman I want. You'll understand some day. No." He stopped under a streetlight. "Understand now. I love you, but not the way I love Amanda. I love her because she is not familiar. Because I don't see myself when I look at her. She has to do with my future, not my past. She is a woman. And you, my dear child, are a girl, my niece. That is wonderful but not the same. . . ."

And then she said the dreadful words she didn't even know she had in her.

"I wanted you to be my father."

"Oh, Sarah." He shook his head. "You aren't going to have that, either. I'm not and won't ever be John Andrew. Never. . . ."

"Why? Oh, why?" Sarah didn't know why she wanted so much and couldn't seem to have it, any of it. First it was Daddy who had chosen to leave her, chosen not to love her, and now it was Uncle Marsh who didn't choose her. It was so much worse than not being chosen at the party.

"It isn't that I don't love you, Sarah. You're growing into a woman that somebody, a man, will love the way you need. I

138

can already see that. Can you let me be your uncle, someone who likes to have you around? Someone who knows you will fall in love some day and you'll be loved back? Can you learn to wait?"

And then he hugged her again, and again she felt the warmth of his hands through her dress and how he smelled like air or water. She sobbed aloud, and it seemed her voice reverberated like bells against the side of the mountain and against the walls of houses. They were close to the church now and she looked at the tall spire, dimly white in the night sky, the shape of the bell silent and still.

❧ 23 ❧

Uncle Marsh went down the stone walk, down the side of the hill, and this time Sarah did not wonder where he was going. She stood outside on the front walk for a moment before she went in to face Mama. The house, surrounded by dark trees and the mountain, had a light burning in every room. It was as though Mama had to have light to comfort herself.

"I declare," she said. "You're back. I simply do not know what gets into you. Weren't you enjoying yourself? Looks to me like you'd want to say something to somebody before you run off like that?"

"Yes'm."

"Weren't you enjoying yourself?"

"It wasn't that. I was—"

Mama didn't wait for her to finish, and Sarah was relieved because she wasn't going to tell her about Miss Bennet and Uncle Marsh or Keziah, either one.

"Then," Mama said, "was there something wrong with the way I planned the party?"

"No. No, ma'm."

"Sarah, look at me." She said that, but she was the one to turn away and look at something else. She picked up two cloudy ice-cream dishes and stacked them into each other. Peach ice cream slopped over onto her fingers. She sucked at them one at a time, and in between sucks she said, "What have I . . . done that was . . . not right? Couldn't you be . . . more polite? I do declare . . . Sarah." Mama looked so frazzled, so hot and tired. Sarah looked over Mama's shoulder into Uncle Marsh's dark, empty room. She saw the scene again, Uncle Marsh and Miss Bennet, as if in a chiaroscuro painting at the art museum. One of those paintings done by Rembrandt with contrasting lights and shades in a room lit palely by one single lamp. Oh, if she could just tell Mama about it. Maybe she could explain everything.

"Sarah, can't you say something? What did I do or not do to make you behave this way? Looks like there's just no pleasin' you."

Why did Mama have to think that everything that happened was because of her? Why did she blame herself for every little thing? Sarah drew back the questions about Uncle Marsh, widened her nostrils to take them all back, breathed them in like a strange scent before she asked them. She breathed out again raggedly and said, "I'm sorry."

She found the silver tray still filled with the Identify items. She put the record needle into the cabinet, the tiny leather-covered book of *Poe's Tales* onto the shelf, and the rubber band into the desk. She threw the lump of coal into the stove. Together, she and Mama straightened up the house and put dirty dishes on the sink board for Keziah to do in the morning.

"I'm sorry, Mama." Sarah said it again. And she was, sorry for Mama. She had worked hard for the party, made her the pink dress with the little capes over the shoulders instead of sleeves, the sweetheart neckline. She'd thought up all the games and tried to make everyone have a good time.

"I'll call Beth Ann and everyone. I'll tell her. If you want me to."

But Mama said, "What's done is done," and she went up to bed.

The next morning Keziah had washed the party things and was frying eggs for breakfast when Sarah got up. Sarah took grits from the pan on the stove and it was a gray-faced, silent Keziah who put an egg on her plate. Sarah sat across the table from Uncle Marsh, who read the paper as he ate. She watched his hands, watched them hold his fork, raise it to his lips, light a cigarette, fold his napkin. Now that he had touched Miss Bennet, she thought his hands would be altered, but she knew, somehow, in the deepest part of her that nothing was changed.

No, something was changed. Uncle Marsh had changed in the way he treated her. She knew that—and it wasn't just last night. When she first came to Hanlon he acted as if she was the most important thing in his life, acted as if she was a grown-up person, let her drink beer with him out of salty glasses and told her about hell. Now he seemed as far away as a movie star, smiling out of the pages of *Photoplay* magazine or from the colored posters in the lobby of the picture show.

Uncle Marsh left for the newspaper office and Sarah sat out on the back porch watching Keziah, inside at the table alone with her breakfast. Keziah bowed her head. She always did this to give thanks to the Lord for her food, dedicated to His good. But she didn't finish her prayer or look up or pick up her fork. She knows I am out here, Sarah thought, and she's waiting for me to leave. Sarah was close enough to see beads of perspiration on Keziah's upper lip. They glistened. *She knows I am here, right enough. Keziah knows every footstep in this house, where it is going, every nuance of voice and what it left unsaid, every smell we have and how we got it. Keziah runs this place. Doesn't she anticipate everything we want or do not want? Doesn't she know I am waiting?*

Sarah couldn't understand Keziah's scorn. The church had been so light, so full of music and energy, some new kind of power. How could it be wrong for her to be part of that? Wasn't church supposed to be God's house? That's what Mr. Hackley in Detroit and Mr. Simpson here said it was. It was God's house, the house of many mansions, and *if it were not so I would have told you.* Sarah repeated the words to herself.

"Keziah, ma'am." Keziah did not look up. "Keziah, isn't your church the house of God?"

"Ha. You know it surely is." Keziah picked up her fork.

"Well, then"—and now Sarah's voice broke into pieces and turned into tears—"why can't I come in?"

"Oh, baby. Oh, *baby!* Come here to me." Keziah opened her arms and took Sarah into them and Sarah cried and smelled Keziah's warm, spicy cinnamon smell. "Hush now. Hush," she said.

"Some people," Keziah said later, after Sarah told her about Uncle Marsh, "some people are like some old man settin' at the supper table—eatin' ever' bite outta a whole big bowl of beans. Leavin' biscuit 'n' tomato 'n' blackberry pie without tastin' any of it. He just eat and eat them beans 'till he bust and then he never eat 'em again. Maybe then, another time, he try the pie."

Sarah leaned into Keziah's body and let her stroke her hair.

"Somebody I know like that. He dig in so deep sometime, just one thing at a time. Leave all the rest."

"You talking about Uncle Marsh?"

"You reckon? Well, one time it was a whole big family of furriners, up at Colco Camp. Took 'em to church, taught 'em how to talk. Slept up there right with 'em at the coal camp. 'Makin' 'em feel welcome,' he said. He like to have eat them people *alive* before he was through."

"Mama said he got lice from the boy."

"Yes, and who was the one had to shave his poor old head?" Keziah said. "Well—and then he run out of juice. Seem like he wore himself *out*."

"It wasn't the war? His scars?"

"Hunhh! Naw, chile, that's how come he *got* them scars. Love his mammy. Then love his pappy. Never both at once. . . ."

"I don't understand. I thought he—"

"Don't think about it. Don't try. You wear yourself out over it. Just like his mammy."

"But—"

"Don't but me no buts, just take him like he is. . . . That's what she does."

"Who?"

"Who? You act like you was an owl. You know who. Miss Amanda. That's who. . . ."

Sarah remembered how Miss Bennet mooned over him, how she showed him her school books and her college test papers written in her curling, round knotted hand; how she laughed up at him and sat so close to him when he helped her with her schoolwork.

"You see her? Lean across him so slow? Wave at people so they know she's ridin' in his big car?" Keziah put her hands on her hips and prissied around, imitating Miss Bennet.

"She asks him about his dreams sometimes," Sarah said, remembering how Miss Bennet asked him whether a man named Freud had ever analyzed his dreams while he was in Europe.

"He don't know nuthin' about dreams. She'll find out."

They went outside and sat on the back-porch steps in the sun, sat there with Sarah curved in Keziah's big body until the telephone rang. Sarah didn't want to leave Keziah's arms, but it was somebody wanting her to come home right quick. Her mama, Aunt Sude, was at it again, and she was sick, too, they said. As Keziah hurried away, she told Sarah to finish up the kitchen.

Now, even though Mama was still upstairs asleep, Sarah felt better. Keziah had let her ask the questions, talked to her about Uncle Marsh. It wasn't that she understood him any better. It was that she knew he was like that all the time, with everyone, even Grandmama, and, she supposed, with Mama, too, once when they were younger. Still, she had to get used to this new thought. First it was Daddy she'd had to get used to. Now it was Uncle Marsh. How she wanted him to be the way she had imagined him! How she wanted him to take her father's place somehow! Still, he was here every day. He had promised to take her over to Virginia to see the fiery coke ovens some night. Sarah sat on the window seat waiting for Mama to wake up. She thought about O-lan, the peasant woman in *The Good Earth*. Miss Bennet had let her read it. O-lan had given up so much.

There was a knock on the screen door and then the bell rang softly. It was Peter who stood there, a sweater tied around his neck, his yellow shirt flicking his cheek in the breezy morning.

❧ 24 ❧

"Hi," he said. One finger traced the curliqued carving on the screen door.

"Hi." She copied his movement along the shape of curved wood on the other side, feeling the fine wire mesh on her finger tips.

"You've got little squares on your face and all over your shirt," he said. She looked down and saw how the sun shining through the wire mesh of the screen left squares reflected onto her white shirt. She felt the prickly, flat nap of the Oriental rug, dry and cool, beneath her bare feet. The sun was high and hot and already glittered into Peter's glasses.

He put his hands in his pockets. "I wondered. You want to go swimming up at Table Rock? With me? Now?"

She shrugged. "I don't know." He seemed different now. As if they shared something, she didn't know what. Peter's old Model T Ford sat at the curb. She thought about Mama sleeping upstairs and Keziah gone down to her mother's house.

"Sure." She shrugged again. "Let's go."

"I'm ready. Just put your bathing suit on under your clothes. I've got us a lunch."

Sarah wrote a note to her mother telling her where Keziah was and that she had gone swimming with Peter. She put her red knitted bathing suit on under her new beach pajamas that Uncle Marsh had bought and pinned the note to the screen door with a bent safety pin.

She liked walking along the railroad tracks in the heat of the day, stepping on every other tie, matching her stride to Peter's. She liked feeling the wide legs of her red-and-white beach pajamas flap against her legs. Black creosoted ties shone in the sun as she walked on the rails, wavering, balancing herself with outstretched arms. The narrow, shining rails of warm metal disappeared around the curved roadbed.

Peter stopped and set the lunch basket down. "Hey," he said, "I want to tell you something. I shouldn't have run out on you last night. I should have stayed."

"It's okay," she said.

"No. I should have stayed. You get in trouble or anything?"

She shook her head. "Uh-uh. Mama just doesn't talk to me. Keziah and Uncle Marsh . . . they're okay, I guess."

"I get whipped."

Peter's face reddened all the way past his ears where his hair was shaved around his head and the skin was white and defenseless through the shaved-off hair. The wind blew his hair, brown as tobacco leaves, every which way like long grass in a field. His yellow shirt collar still flipped the edge of his chin and his full lips pressed over his teeth, almost too big for his face. There were fine light hairs on his arms and she watched them move in the breeze. Sarah wondered if Peter's father made him cut a switch the way Mama used to do, or made him pull his pants down the way Keziah did to James. Sometimes, Keziah said, James couldn't sit down in school for a week after she used a leather belt on him.

"I wanted to run away last night," Sarah said looking down the tracks. "Even before we went to Keziah's church."

"Where to?"

"Back home, Detroit."

"You couldn't. You—"

"Plenty of kids do it. I've read about them. I could. They have kids our age in shanty towns, in shacks under bridges."

"Maybe. But maybe you'd end up like that boy, then."

"What boy?"

"A boy Father told me about. He hopped a train. Fell off when guards chased him. The train cut his head . . . off." Peter made a slicing motion across his neck. "Eyes still open. Cut it clean."

"How you talk! You know in your heart that is not the cross-your-heart-hope-to-die everlasting truth."

"Sure, it's the truth. Father told me. Policeman told him. He had to pick it up. The head, I mean. The policeman, I mean."

Holding hands lightly across the smooth, blue tracks, they balanced themselves by leaning away from each other in a *V.* The bright towels Sarah carried billowed from her opposite arm like banners. The tracks were ribbons, she thought, undulating all across the country, leading them somewhere, anywhere, maybe Hollywood or out where the cowboys were.

"If you keep on up that way"—Peter pointed a thumb up the tracks—"there's a train tunnel. They blasted it right through the center of the mountain. I'll take you home that way if you want to."

She smiled at him. "And I'll show you my Aunt Wanda Raines' house up that way—just past the tunnel."

They turned into a narrow path leading through sun-filtered woods.

❧ 25 ❧

The pool was a deep, wide, wild place in the river with broad, flat rocky outcroppings along one side like a table. It was on the flat table-rock they put their towels and basket of lunch. On the opposite side of the pool there rose a sheer cliff of granite. Woods atop the cliff and round the pool were green and blue, black and purple. Dappled yellow sunshine filtered through leaves onto the forest floor, moving, flickering, turning in the wind. Below them, around a bend in the river, were the low falls. Sarah heard the river sounds, the water falling, the trees sighing and above that, birds.

Peter took off his glasses. Sarah liked the shape of his head, his neat hair. She stared at the muscles on his arms and chest, defined in a way that hers were not. She looked away when he unbuttoned his trousers, stepped out of them and dove into the water. She watched as he swam to the farthest edge of the swimming place, his white-green body like marble beneath the water's surface, wavy and unclear. At the rock wall, he clambered out, hitched up his swimming suit and hollered at her, but the sound of water carried his words away.

They played all morning in the pool, racing each other from stone to stone. She swam underwater until she could hold her breath no longer, emerging from foaming water to lie on the table of rock and sun herself. Propped up on her elbow, lying on her side, she talked to him, talked more than she had talked the first time, and he told her about his mother. She still could not say everything about her father. They ate hard-boiled eggs and cold fried chicken with bread and butter and sweet pickles Peter's grandmother fixed. The sun was hotter than before, and Sarah stretched out to let sun steep into her. She felt like a lizard soaking up enough warmth for the whole day, soaking up energy and life. She squinted into the sunshine, looked at Peter from beneath her eyelids. The white knitted top of his bathing suit was cut out so that she could see his ribs.

"Hey," she said, "I can count every one of your ribs. Every single one." She sat up and he turned to face her, grinning. "Peter, look, I can. See, I can even see your heart beat."

The skin on his chest swelled and fluttered, swelled and fluttered as his heart pumped in and out. She thought about his red, pulsing heart and what would happen if it suddenly stopped. It was a marvel, she thought. The sight and her thoughts and the sun brought tears to her eyes. She touched the pulsing place with one finger. He wrapped his fingers around her one finger.

"I wish I could see your heart beating, too," he said, looking down at her red woolen breast.

She wanted to die. To curl up like a piece of bacon on this

skillet of hot rock and disappear was all she wanted. She hadn't known that what she said would sound so awful, or how he would answer. She looked a long time at the wishbone she held in her hand. Throwing it into the water, she plunged in head first, wishing she would disappear with it beneath the water forever. When she opened her eyes the rocky walls seemed to waver like tremors of heat above a fire and he was there beside her, laughing. He blew bubbles in the throbbing water and everything was a different shape and sound. When they came to the top she heard his words, flung back across his shoulder, fading in the spray.

"I'm sorrreeee! Sorreee!"

Then they swam, elbows rising like arrows above their heads, legs flailing, breathing the watery air. They swam close to the falls, swam close enough to feel the current, strong and insistent. The water became shallower.

"Let's go over." Peter grabbed her arm. "Over the falls!"

She stood up, water running out of her hair and over her shoulders. Water eddied, swirled around her legs, climbing up to run quickly like hands down her body. She let herself be pushed and pulled by the fluid force. Water filled her eyes and mouth and nose. She could not breathe and struggled to stand again.

"Just relax. Let yourself go, go on over."

So they were thrown by the river's intensity, thrown together, his hand on her arm or leg, then her belly, or around her waist; hers caught his head and shoulders, his thighs. They were tumbled like stones into the din of water falling or leaping up and dashing down again into fountains of spray.

Then it was not just tumulous water rising and falling everywhere and their helplessness. It was something more. Some other force seemed to be taking her over. She clung to Peter, both arms around his waist, her head thrown back. He shuddered. The noise, the cold, the falling forever down the long slide of water, his curved arms and legs, shoulders and buttocks and his back with its arch in the center where the backbone grew; she could not stop herself. She kissed him over and over again and he kissed her, his hands holding her face. It was as though they were sea animals coiling around each other, breathless, skin to skin, glistening in the sun, water pouring from heads and shoulders.

They were thrown into the foamy yellow spray below, and Sarah's back and legs scraped against the rough riverbed, and still she held him. They were washed onto a gravel bar at the bottom of the falls. They lay there clinging like barnacles on a reef and she felt his hands moving, his eyes wide open. Finally, he said, "Shall we go over one more time?" and she said, "No, I don't think we should."

❧ 26 ❧

As they walked along the riverbank, she couldn't look at Peter. She felt she had to save herself from him somehow, to prevent that surge of feeling from ever happening again. She'd have to tell him not to come back. She would miss, she thought, the funny quick way he spoke and the way he seemed shy and yet careless at the same time. She would find a way to tell him what she had decided. She bent to take off her shoes, filled with sand and gravel bits.

"Do you still. . . ," he asked first. "What about the tunnel? Still want to go home that way?"

He put his hand on her shoulder. She shrugged, her head down, but his hand stayed there on her shoulder.

"Do you?" she said.

"Sure. If you've never seen one . . . might as well."

"Okay." A long pause. "Okay, yes, sure."

They walked along the sandy path and Sarah turned to look back at their footprints in the soft sand together, his large and deep, hers light and shallow. She carried her thin-soled shoes as the wind swooped down into the little valley and blew her hair away from her face. Above her, sun shone into one-eyed old mine openings up on the hillsides. Sarah remembered blackened men in rough, wet clothes. She'd seen them at Marsh's mine wearing carbide lamps on their foreheads, handloading coal onto carts in rain.

They came to steep embankments rising on either side of the train tracks making a narrow cut between hills not much wider than the tracks. She heard singing, voices coming down to them as if from a stage suspended in the sky.

"When I was young and in my prime
I thought I would never marry. I fell in love with a pretty little girl. . . ."

Happy voices singing, picnickers, perhaps, in the woods above them. Sarah looked into the feathery trees edging the sand trail.

"Sure enough, we got married."

Two voices, clear and sweet.

"Rinktum, dinktum, tarry.
Prettiest little girl in all the world
And her name was Devilish Mary."

She could see them now. Two figures, a man and a woman, hand in hand coming down the hill toward the tunnel. It was Mama and Bay.

"If ever I marry for the second time
It'll be for love not riches.
I'll marry one about two feet high
So she can't wear my britches."

Mama didn't look like herself. What was it? Of course she smiled up at Bay, carried his precious notebooks as she always did now, but it was something more, something around her face. She caught sight of Sarah and Peter and waved. Sarah knew she had already forgotten all about last night and how Sarah was supposed to be in disgrace.

"Hey!" Mama shouted. "What're y'all doin' way up here?" Now she was close enough for Sarah to see what it was that was so different. It was her hair. All her beautiful, long, red hair that Daddy called her crowning glory was gone. It was as if Mama had cut Daddy right out of her life for good now.

As they walked along, Mama told Sarah that she and Bay had been up the mountain to Miss May Hopkins' cabin.

"Miss May? I knew she could if she would, she could sing verses Bay had never heard before. We left our car right up there on the road next to yours."

Mama didn't mention her hair and it wasn't as though she didn't have it on her mind, either. She felt the back of her head as if she were looking for the heavy knot there and shook her head to see why it was so light and free.

Finally she said, "I feel so light-headed with my hair all gone. It's a wonderful, flyaway feeling. Do you like it, honey?" she said and looked out of her almond eyes.

"I don't know. I can't . . . I can't get used to it, Mama."

Why do you have to ask me that? Why do you have to make everything different? What about Daddy?

Sarah felt dark and thin and frazzled next to Mama's golden, sunshiney look. She certainly didn't look as if she might die, as Mrs. Drisdon had warned—not anymore, not since Bay Arnett had come.

"After you and Keziah left this morning, I was up at the house alone and Bay came and"—Mama's words rushed out and she almost skipped in the sand—"and then he cut it for me. I'd just washed it and was out in the yard letting it dry.

157

You know how long it takes to dry? Well, he just picked up one strand of hair and . . ." she made a motion with her hand, "snipped it off!"

Mama looked amazed, as if she herself could not quite believe what had happened. "Then, of course, we had to just keep going." Bayliss Arnett laughed out loud.

Sarah saw the scene in her mind's eye.

"You want to look like all the others? Those men-women dancin' at the black-and-tans?"

It was Daddy talking, his black eyes hard as coal and glittery.

"God gave you that hair and it's a sin even to think about cuttin' it."

"But it takes so long to dry," Mama said. "It turns sour sometimes."

Daddy would not relent. . . . "Kneel down," he said. "Kneel. Dry it in the oven."

So Mama knelt down on a rag rug in front of the oven, laid a towel on the door, and stayed that way with Daddy watching from the kitchen door, his arms folded across his chest, as she combed, fingered, brushed her hair until it was dry. Sarah saw it from the dining room and was afraid of the whiteness of her mother's neck with all the hair combed up, afraid of the smell of burning hair.

Peter led the way toward the tunnel opening that was cut through solid rock into the mountain. Sarah followed Bay and Mama inside. Her eyes widened. Coming out of the brilliant sunshine and wind into the still, cool tunnel, she could not see, only smelled wet earth and rock. There was no sound inside except their footsteps, echoing. Mama walked along carefully, stepping along the cinder path from tie to tie, rubbing the small of her back with one hand, the other clutching Bay's notebooks to her.

"Y'all don't know no songs ner nothin', do ye?"

Bay tried to speak the old Scots-Irish dialect, the way people talked in the mountains, the people who gave him their songs. Mama and Peter said, "Well, I don't know. What shall we sing? You decide."

Bay started. "Oh, many a man's been murdered by the railroad, the rail—"

Mama stopped him. "Don't," she said. "Please do not sing that. I'm wary of this place anyhow. That song doesn't help one bit."

In a minute Peter crowed like a rooster and the echoing "doodley-doo" made them laugh. Mama sang then, her scales and vocalizations, "*may, mee, moh, mah, moooooo,*" and the walls answered her. The cavern was filled with sound as they swung easily from tie to tie or balanced on the tracks.

Mama stopped once or twice and waited for Sarah to catch up. When she paused she put both hands around the small of her back and stretched herself for a moment, but she kept up with Bay and kept singing.

Sarah was still barefoot, her shoes tied together around her neck. She and Peter balanced on the train tracks as they had on the way to swim earlier. He looked at her as if he'd already forgotten going over the falls together. But she knew she would never forget.

Rising above their voices there was a new sound, distant, unmistakable.

"That wasn't the train?" Mama said it as if she knew very well it was. "What time is it? It's way past time for the . . ."

"My God, I think we're going to have to run for it," Bay said. Sarah started to run, turned and ran the other way, turned again.

"No! Sarah!" Mama screamed it. "The train's coming that way!" Her voice reverberated against the tunnel and the walls answered, "way-ay-ay!"

"Run!" Peter grabbed Sarah's hand. He dropped the heavy picnic basket and pulled Sarah along with him. As they ran along the tracks, cinders cut into Sarah's feet but she couldn't stop now to put her shoes on. In the weak light still coming in at them from the tunnel mouth Sarah saw Bay helping Mama. He looked lopsided, like a crab scuttling along a log. The sound of the train was louder now and the walls seemed to waver.

"Stop a minute! Lucey! You can't run!" Bay shouted. "The baby! You can't! We'll get you in one of those places in the wall."

He pointed to a small place along the wall big enough for a person to stand, pushed her toward it. "Let the train pass you by. . . ."

"No!" Mama screamed and ran down the tracks away from all of them standing there. "I'd rather die!" Mama screamed back at them.

"Run!" Peter pulled at Sarah.

Mama said she'd rather die. For the first time, Sarah thought maybe they would all die in there with the train. She shuddered and ran on, her feet slamming into the rough cinders, pain reaching like knives up her legs, into her spine. What if Mama did die? Now. What if she, Sarah died, too? Oh, why hadn't she gone upstairs this morning? Gone into Mama's room to say she was sorry for leaving the party, for having the spell right on the front porch that time? Why hadn't she loved Mama enough? She watched her mother run, limping now, bent at the waist as if something hurt her. Oh, what about the baby?

❧ 27 ❧

Suddenly their space was filled with more light and more noise than she could have imagined. Air was sucked out of the tunnel. It grew hotter and Sarah couldn't see Mama.

"Mama! Please! It's in here with us. Get me out!"

Sarah sobbed and stumbled. Mama turned, pulled at her, while Bay half carried, half pushed them toward the opening. *Oh, how far is it?* Peter helped Mama and they all ran that way until Mama fell and took Peter down with her onto the tracks. The train thundered on toward them, closer and closer.

"Leave me! Oh! Leave . . . Sarah!" Mama screamed and yet Sarah could barely hear her words. "My baby! My poor orphan child!"

They pulled her to her feet and dragged themselves toward the precious light, which shone in at them now like honey.

The great roar of engine blotted out everything in Sarah's brain. Nothing existed except the engine with its hot smell of iron and water steaming onto the ground rushing beneath the wheels. Sarah struggled as if under water in some deep, deep place, struggled to get to sweet light and silence. The whistle blew as she threw herself out of the tunnel's black maw in a horrible birthing. She fell down a gravel bank, felt steam on her leg, felt Mama catch her, hold her.

It seemed as long as life before the last empty coal car clattered past them. They lay there, Mama breathing into her face. Peter and Bay, farther down the embankment stared up at them. The blessed silence, silence was all she heard and Mama breathing. The pain in Sarah's feet bloomed and receded, bloomed again like bubbles in a thick boiling pot. A wide blister raised itself on her leg; the skin broke and fell away like a curtain. She looked at it. It seemed to belong to someone else, it was not hers.

Mama got up on her hands and knees, her face white as steam, her hair chopped and stiff around her face. She had Bay's notebook in one hand.

"Sarah! My God, Bay, look at her leg! Oh!" Mama stood up, her hands spread like fans against her body. They all knew without speaking that it was Mama's baby. Something was about to happen that should not be happening yet.

They decided Bay would go on up to the next hollow to find Aunt Wanda Raines and bring her to help Mama.

"She's a granny woman, Mama. And she can stop blood and fire."

"A midwife," Bay said. "All right, then. I'll be back as quick as I can."

"I'll go on back to the car, Miz Raines. I'll get you the doctor. And Sarah. . . ." Peter started down the tracks.

"Marsh," Mama said. "Call Marsh."

Sarah crawled away from the tracks, found a flat place nearby and leaned against the mossy trunk of a beech tree. Her feet throbbed and her blistered skin hung loosely away from her leg like a burst balloon. Mama walked back and forth on the flat rock as Peter disappeared down the railroad. Bay was already out of sight around the curve of mountain above them. There was no sound in the tunnel and only the engine's mournful call could be heard across the valley.

"How ironic," Mama spoke in her Detroit voice now, so Sarah knew she was trying to do something she didn't want to. "How strange that I need Wanda Raines after all this time. She was so. . . ."

"Crazy, Mama? You always say that, but she's not."

"Sarah, you take things so seriously. Not crazy, really, just well . . . queer."

"Way back before your daddy and I married, when we were courtin', if. . . ," she said, sighing, "if that is what you could call it, Wanda came into Hanlon one time and told me to let him be."

Pain appeared on Mama's face like a moon shadow. She rocked back and forth before she went on. It seemed to Sarah that she had to tell this story before the baby could be born.

"She wore one of those poke bonnets? All you could see was her cheekbones, like great moons they were, loomin' out of her face. And she speaks in that, well, you know, *passionate* voice."

"'He's got a darkness in him,'" she told me. "'You been way off over yonder to school and such. He can't even read hardly. There's not a blessed thing in this world he can give you. . . .'"

Mama made a queer sound in the back of her throat and pressed her hands against her mouth. She continued her story in a quick way of speaking, hurrying.

"Wanda said, 'Besides, he's not . . . right. Never will be. Not since that war took his brothers and not him.' But I knew she was wrong and so was Papa. He was right, right for me and I married him."

Sarah remembered her father's sadness and Mama stopped talking for awhile. Then, in a minute she said, "Hurry. Oh, hurry."

In a little while it was too late.

"The baby's coming and there's no one here but us, honey."

Mama told Sarah they'd need something clean to wrap the baby in. Clean as they could find. So they tore off Mama's skirt and she had to lie there in her petticoat while Sarah tore the skirt in two pieces.

"I wish . . . I wish you didn't have to do all this. See this," Mama said. She was panting now.

"What shall I do? I have to help. How can we? Will it die out here? And you, too?" Sarah was so afraid that she could not think. She couldn't let Mrs. Drisdon's prophecy come true.

"Sarah, I am not going to die. You can hold my hand."

Sarah tried to stand up. The pain in her torn feet and burned leg forced her back onto the ground. She reached out her hand to Mama.

*   *   *

To bring the baby, Mama squatted over the clean cloth they had smoothed over the ground. When it was over, Sarah wrapped the baby in the second piece of cloth and put the little bundle on Mama's lap as she lay propped against a tree to wait. She sat there in the hot sun, the baby on her lap, the birthing cord still pulsating into the baby's body, her blood soaking into the earth. By the time she brought the spongy, purplish afterbirth, flies had already swarmed around her and a blue jay circled above, squawking his raucous warning that something terrible had happened.

❧ 28 ❧

Mama said, "I knew it. All the time. Well, all right."

Aunt Wanda told Mama the baby didn't breathe, not even one time, and he had red hair just like hers.

Mama waved her arm, pushing Aunt Wanda away. "Look at Sarah," she said. "She's . . . burned."

Mama dropped her head back against the tree, her new bangs damp and stringy across her forehead. Sarah couldn't see Mama's eyes but knew they were empty—the way they'd been that night Daddy killed himself. Sarah blinked. It was the first time she had said those words even to herself.

Aunt Wanda kneeled down on the slab of rock, kneeled down on one knee, propped herself on the other leg with both hands on her thigh.

"There's a fire still burnin' in your leg," she said. "I'm a'goin' to blow it out. You recollect the Dockery girl? Emma Jean? And the verse?"

"Yes'm."

"Well, all we got to do is keep that fire from gettin' to the bone. All you got to do, now, is lie still and hush."

Aunt Wanda's lips moved as she mouthed the Bible verse over to herself. Mama looked at the dead child in her lap and held onto the ground beneath her with both hands as if she were going to fly off the face of the earth. Wringing his hands as though they were laundry, Bay walked around in a circle. *His face is young*, Sarah thought. Even when he smokes and smoke drifts into his eyes, he is more like Peter than he is like Uncle Marsh. She felt as old as Bay somehow. Keziah would say that his hair was all skee-wift, and he had blood on his shirt.

"And when I passed by thee, Sarah Raines, and saw thee, polluted in thine own burning, Sarah Raines, I said unto thee, Sarah Raines, when thou wast in thy burning, 'Live!' Yea, I said unto thee, Sarah Raines, when thou wast in thy burning, 'Live!'"

Aunt Wanda passed her hand over Sarah's leg, now oozing yellow liquid. Three times she repeated the verse from Ezekiel. Sarah looked at her aunt's broken fingernails, felt her breath as fragrant as if she'd been eating raspberries, smelled her sweaty, wood-sorrel, coal-stove smell.

Later, after they'd been carried back to Aunt Wanda's and put to bed, Mama wandered out from behind the curtains where she had slept on Aunt Wanda's bed. She smelled of disinfectant, and she stood close to Sarah lying on the big Murphy bed. She didn't look as if she'd just had a baby. Only her hair was changed. But was that really all? What would she do now? Go back to swinging on the front porch for the rest of her natural life? Ignore everything again? Something told Sarah, no, Mama is different now. She belongs here in Hanlon. Mama would never go back to Detroit now.

With Aunt Wanda's hairbrush, Mama brushed at her hair as if she could make it grow long again, as if she were thinking about Daddy and what he would think.

"Does it hurt? Your leg?" she asked.

"No, ma'am. Well, a little."

"Your feet? You're going to have them—the cinders—taken out when we get back to town."

"It's all right, Mama."

Mama went on, "I reckon you'll have a scar there."

Sarah thought about Uncle Marsh. Would her scars look like his?

"Can I do it?" Sarah said.

"Do what, honey?"

"Brush it for you? Your hair?" Sarah remembered Nancy and how they used to sit on her bed and brush each other's hair. Like monkeys in the zoo, Nancy had said. Sarah took the brush, still warm from Mama's hand, counted and pushed the brush through Mama's lustrous hair. She felt a great rise of feeling.

"Mama. I'm sorry. Sorry about the baby. Everything."

"I know," Mama said and smoothed Aunt Wanda's blue bathrobe over and over her knee in little pleats. "Well," she said with a sigh, "what's done is done, I reckon. I reckon the Lord knows what he is doing. Though I do not." She took the brush from Sarah to brush her hair. "I'm . . . I am sorry, too, sorry as I can be."

It was dark outside now and the window was black and closed as the back of a mirror.

"Did you want him, Mama?"

"Want him? Lord, honey. I do not know. No," she shook her head. "Yes. Oh, Sarah. . . ."

"Aren't you even going to give him a name?" Sarah's voice rose. She dared not think about the baby she'd wanted as a friend, about Daddy, about Mama and Bay singing, about his cutting Mama's hair.

Mama lit a cigarette. That was one more thing. Bay had started Mama on cigarettes, and Daddy believed that was for fallen women, too, and Mama didn't even seem to care.

"I tried wanting him. I thought it would make things right."

"Aren't you even going to name him?" Sarah asked again.

"Why don't you?" Mama blew smoke out of her nose and waved it away with her hand. "You name him."

"John Andrew."

"What?"

"John Andrew!"

Mama's face broke into pieces then. It had been smooth and flat and now it was crumpled, broken. She stretched out her arms to Sarah and they held each other, rocking each other back and forth on the bed. Finally Mama said they'd have to have a little funeral. "Aunt Wanda knows what to do. Tomorrow."

"All right. Then I'll put his name in Aunt Wanda's bible with Daddy and you and everybody," Sarah said.

"You put it in like that . . . John Andrew Raines, Junior."

Aunt Wanda brought them cups of tea, made, she said, from the bark of an apple tree close to the house. Mama drank hers and said, "Thank you. Thank you for all you've done today for me and for Sarah. I reckon . . . I've been mean about . . . things. I hope you—"

169

Aunt Wanda interrupted, "Hit don't matter a bit in this world er the next," she said. "We'll just let bygones be bygones, I reckon." And she and Mama looked at each other for a long time.

Now maybe Mama and Aunt Wanda would be friends, Sarah thought. It was as if two parts of her, the Raines part and the Stannard part, had been sewn into one whole piece, like a patchwork quilt, and were all one now.

❧ 29 ❧

When Uncle Marsh and Peter and Keziah got to Aunt
Wanda's for the funeral the next morning, Aunt Wanda had
taken out the worst of the cinders in Sarah's feet while Sarah
hung onto Mama's hand the way Mama had clung to hers the
day before. Bay made a little coffin from some boards of oak
in the shed and Aunt Wanda found a baby blanket to wrap
the baby in.

Keziah came into the small house, and she seemed bigger
and blacker than she did in her rightful place down at Uncle
Marsh's. Keziah stared at everything in Aunt Wanda's room,
the huge folddown bed, the blooming things, and the num-
berless jars catching fire from the sun and throwing it back
onto the floors and the people.

"Glad to see you didn't put no window in that box. They
does that sometimes," she said as if it was all she could think
of. "Just to let ever'body look in and see the dead folks, lyin'
in there." She looked around and smelled the air as if she
were trying to find something that smelled bad in Aunt

Wanda's house. Sarah remembered Daddy's closed-up silent coffin. She thought about him and about his undershirt she had worn so long.

Uncle Marsh and Peter stood on the front porch and watched Bay sweep up the sawdust. They rocked back and forth on their heels, their hands in their pockets, hats pushed off their foreheads. They looked down the road or out into the valley below them.

While Bay and Peter took turns digging a grave, Mama walked around in Aunt Wanda's blue housecoat and Keziah trailed behind her looking glum. Sarah couldn't understand why Keziah acted so stuck-up and snooty but decided she had to think about the funeral and the baby and whether it would ever see their daddy. Uncle Marsh came into the house, tilting his head the way he did, his scars shining purple.

Sarah pointed to the little coffin. "I want to . . ." she hesitated, "put something—a present?—in there with him, with the baby." It had come to her with a flash what she wanted to do. "A gift," she said and told Uncle Marsh about Daddy's undershirt and how she had worn it for protection.

"Nosir! It is not too late, not one minute," he said and made everyone wait while he sped down the mountain in his car, back to Grandmama's room and the top drawer of the highboy.

Then, together, they opened the box and, along with a sick, sweet odor, they found the baby's body wrapped in Aunt Wanda's baby blanket with embroidered flowers on it. Only his blackish face, like an animal's face, peered out of the flap of blanket over his head. Sarah tucked Daddy's undershirt next to the baby. Daddy's smell was faded away now and her smell was strong in it.

"It'll be his little pillow," Uncle Marsh said and then he had the most wonderful gift of all. Into the baby's little hand he put a long coil of Mama's red hair he'd found on the floor of Mama's bedroom. Sarah thought the gifts were the most powerful they could have thought of.

The grave was deep enough. Mama was dressed now and Uncle Marsh put Sarah in a chair Peter had set out in the yard. Aunt Wanda picked bellflowers, campanula she called them, and Uncle Marsh put the box in the ground while Aunt Wanda said words over it. As she repeated "dust thou art" Sarah wondered if Mama would fall onto the grave again. She did not, only leaned forward to put the violet-blue bellflowers into the grave just as Keziah threw a handful of dirt down onto the little box. Keziah cleared her throat and blew her nose on a man's big handkerchief.

"If they was to ring the bell down there at the First Methodist, how many passing bells you reckon they'd toll for such a little bitty thing?" she said.

❧ 30 ❧

The first thing Sarah did when Dr. Spidell told her she could walk again was to take a bowl of rice pudding down to Aunt Sude, Keziah's mother. Today Aunt Sude sat on a cane-bottom chair in the dirt yard combing her hair. Her blue knotted scarf lay on the ground beside her.

"I can still comb my own head," she said.

"I see you can. That's fine, Aunt Sude." Sarah sat on the front stoop hoping this wasn't going to be one of her bad days. "Aunt Sude? I brought you some of Mama's rice pudding. That old recipe of hers?" And then she remembered. Mama said it was Aunt Sude's recipe first. But Sarah didn't mention it. It was all too complicated to explain to the old woman.

"Huh!" Aunt Sude spit in the yard. "Which one are you?"

"Sarah Stannard Raines? You remember."

"Raines! Huh! You ain't one of them?" Aunt Sude stopped combing her little tufts of hair. The soft fringe around her face and ears was white, but where she'd rubbed all the hair off the top of her head, only stiff bristles remained. Her dark skull shone through the rough stubble like a man's new beard. She stopped her combing and began to rub her head, chewing that invisible something she always chewed. A rooster, all cinnamon and blue and red, galloped across the clean-swept yard, his feet as big as fans from McMaury's Funeral Parlor.

"My father was a Raines," Sarah began. She had to go through this every time she visited Aunt Sude.

"I knows who you is," Aunt Sude said, rubbing that spot in her head in a circular motion.

Sarah took her ash-colored hand into hers. "You oughtn't to do that way," she said.

"You're the one's daddy killed hisself."

Sarah dropped Aunt Sude's hand as if it were afire.

"He wa'n't no 'count. Made moonshine. Had a child too soon. Went North. Drank whiskey ag'in the law. Shot hisself in the head. Brains come—"

Sarah covered her mouth with her hand and turned away from the old woman. She felt again the muffled shot across in the park, saw Daddy sprawled and jerking. She stumbled up from the steps. How dare that old woman talk to her that way? Well, she could just sit there and rub herself bald. She wasn't going to sit there and listen even if Keziah and Mama had told her not to pay Aunt Sude's outbursts any mind. She couldn't ignore her words. Out in the dusty road, her feet sank in the powder and made a quiet, thick sound. The rooster with its red wattles flopping followed her. She should shoo it back into the yard but didn't care.

"And missy," Aunt Sude hooted after Sarah, "how long

you think you and your mama goin' to stay up there with Mr. Marsh? Huh?"

Sarah hurried down River Road, past little ramshackle houses. From the bridge arched over the river she looked down at the Holiness Church, silent now. It didn't have a bell, she thought, hurrying along the riverbank. The river was flat and gray as a plate. No wind blew little waves on the water, no sun sprinkled its diamonds over the surface. Water darkened the rocks lying on shore and made a fingering noise against the roots of trees. Sarah sat down on a tree root, that old knot in her belly tied up again. Aunt Sude had said terrible things about her father's life. Even if Mama was right when she said Aunt Sude had been holding in a lot of hate so long that it just overflowed on to anyone who happened to be in the way, even so, was this Daddy's real story, after all? Surely he was more than that. She remembered how he worked in Mama's roses, bending to drink in their sweet smell.

"Made moonshine. Had a child too soon. Drank whiskey and shot hisself."

Where were the stories about his music and how he liked his house with a real bathroom and how he loved Mama? Why hadn't Mama told his real story? Why hadn't *she?* Was it because she wasn't sure how she felt? Wasn't sure she could remember the good things? Maybe Uncle Marsh was right when he first told her that heaven or hell was right here, right now. If she could forget the darkness, maybe then John Andrew's story would not have to be the hateful one told by Aunt Sude.

But what could she do? How could she tell the other story?

She picked up a stone, threw it into the river, and watched

176

silver circles radiate outward. She threw another. These newer circles touched the first, shivering them into different, messy paths. But the first, the farthest rings continued, growing as they ran to the opposite shore. Sarah told herself her father's life was like that. Some of it broken and wrong; some clean and perfect. She knew somehow she'd have to be the one to tell the truth.

She heard the church bell ring, Grandmama's bell in the belfry of the Methodist Church. She stood up and turned toward home. The bellsong had sent her a message.

❧ 31 ❧

It was the middle of the night, but there they were, walking up Laurel Street on their way to church, big as life and twice as natural, Mama said. It wasn't Wednesday night prayer meeting or Sunday morning services, but there they were. The moon followed along with them like a roly-poly dog on a string while Sarah told Mama her plan. Well, just a little part of it because that was the only way she got Mama to get up out of bed and go with Sarah in the first place.

"I'm not going back . . . to Detroit. You can if you want." Sarah talked to the back of her mother's skirt as she walked a few steps ahead in the moon's path. The moon was bright enough to cast shadows on Mama's skirt as it moved into light and then dark like a curtain. "I'll just stay here with Uncle Marsh. Or Aunt Wanda. Keziah, maybe?"

"You know you can't stay with Marsh. What about Amanda? They wouldn't want another person around them," Mama said, but Sarah knew good and well that Mama didn't think Uncle Marsh was going to get married to anybody.

"We could go on down to the Honeymoon Cottage and trade with her," Sarah said.

"I reckon we could."

"He's over in Knoxville, Mama. She's here."

"Yes'm. That's what I mean," Mama said.

They walked to the corner of Center Street.

"He's over there talkin' to people about the TVA. Somebody whose land'll be flooded out. Buried under water so we can have electricity," Mama said. "He says he wants to actually live over there. Be on the spot when the water comes in. Take pictures."

"Like the time with the Hungarian miners?" Sarah asked.

"Yes, I reckon," Mama said. "Like that. He's got him a new cause."

They were getting closer to the church. When Mama asked Sarah if she was sure she didn't want to go back to Detroit, Sarah shook her head.

"I like it here," she began. "I like . . . the way it smells."

Now why in the world did she say that of all things? There were so many things she liked, and she'd been waiting so long to tell Mama. She'd been afraid to admit that she hardly missed home at all. Her letters to Nancy were no longer messages of loneliness but patient, studied answers to dutiful letters from her best friend. Out of sight, out of mind, Keziah said about it. But Uncle Marsh said, no, it was because people change and grow.

"I like the way people know who I am, who we are. You know, we're the Raineses and the Stannards all mixed together. I like Uncle Marsh and Keziah. Aunt Wanda Raines." And now, Peter, she thought, and her little flowerdy room and the high windows looking out on the mountains. Mostly, the mountains and the way they seemed to hold her, hunker down around her in a circle.

"Are we? Going back, I mean?"

"Not if you don't want to," Mama said, and Sarah thought then that she loved Mama more than she ever knew. How could she have hated her sometimes and ignored her so often?

"I've been wanting to say something to you about it. I can sell the house. Mrs. Drisdon's brother? I have an idea he'll live there. She can keep on eye on him instead of us." Mama smiled. "More'n likely, I will never get a better offer. Not in these times. So if you say the word, I'll tell her yes."

The moon hid itself behind a cloud for a moment.

"But what about my books? All the furniture and things?"

"We'll get them. Uncle Marsh doesn't want us to worry about that part. You see, Bay says . . . he says I could sing. Travel all over the state, all over the South, maybe. Sing for money, Sarah." Mama's eyes gleamed.

Rain fell without warning into the dust. Drops of water made soft thunks slowly in the dusty street. Sarah watched the big drops paint the cobblestones one at a time and she wondered how it could rain and shine at the same time, even if it was moonshine.

"I've been a mighty good sport about this for too long, Sarah. I think it's time you told me why you got me up out of bed."

"We're going in the church. Now," Sarah said. She took Mama's hand.

"Nobody's up there this time of night. You're. . . ." Sarah knew Mama would have said 'crazy' before . . . before the baby and Aunt Wanda's help, but she stopped.

"I know," Sarah said.

"Sarah, I believe you have lost your mind," Mama did say.

"Yes," Sarah said and she knew now she was out of her mind, out of the mind that wouldn't remember the good story about Daddy, wouldn't forgive him for choosing to die, choosing not to live with her, with Mama. She was out of the mind that wanted to make Uncle Marsh over into something she would never have again.

The church was white as milk in the moonlight. Tall windows with arches on top were black and dense. An open tree sprinkled heart-shaped leaf shadows over the double front doors as Sarah put her hand on the door.

"Keziah found me this old key. Said it was yours once." Sarah whispered. "You reckon it still works?"

The key turned in the lock and the door swung open. They went on in and it was just as though it was a Sunday morning with the preacher standing in the doorway to greet the congregation, all with their Bible study books in their hands. Sarah pulled Mama up the aisle with her.

"Sarah. This is the last time. What *are* we doing here?" Mama looked pleased to be in on it, whatever she thought it might be. "You tell me what you're lookin' so mysterious about!"

"You'll see."

Sarah kept on, right past the altar and the pulpit without one glance at Grandmama's stained glass windows.

"If it is not to kneel at the altar, where in the world are you takin' me? I am not going to take another step." Mama pulled back on Sarah's shoulder. But Sarah continued across the church and up a short flight of steps into the small room beneath the church bell tower. Mama followed.

The belfry above them smelled of dry leaves and iron and musty birds and their lime. Out of the latticework Sarah saw rooftops and Big Black Mountain as solid as the earth. Streets gleamed in the moonlight and trees were black circles against walkways. When she saw the bell, Sarah's face shone and Mama's almond eyes were full of moon.

"Ring it!" Sarah demanded, pointing to the bell pull.

"Oh, honey."

"Go on, ring it thirty-nine times for Daddy. One ring for every year he lived. It is right, Mama."

Mama laughed then, her laugh rising, breaking, rising again like swallows in flight.

"We'll wake the whole town."

"I know."

Sarah put her hands on Mama's face as if she were the child.

"If it's right to ring the bell when Uncle Marsh came back from France alive, it's right to ring it now for Daddy," she said.

"Go on, then," Mama said. "Pull it for John Andrew."

"I'll do nineteen. You do twenty. You go first."

"No. I want you to ring it first."

A sudden bird flapped its wings above their heads and Sarah started at the noise. She took the rope, worn soft and pliable with many hands, many ringings. At first hesitantly and then with soaring exuberance, she pulled the rope and tolled the bell, the passing bell. Down she pulled and her knees bent and then the bell rolled up and her arms jerked up with it. It seemed her shoulder bones would pull out of their sockets. Sound filled her eyes and mouth.

One, two . . . three . . . four. The bell swung back and forth and she remembered the paper dolls, all holding hands, her father had cut out for her. *Seven . . . eight . . . nine.* She pulled, letting the weight lift her onto her toes and then let her squat down on her heels. Clanging around her head, filling the belfry, the bell touched the mountains with sound. The bell sound blocked out the rest of the world and Sarah could only remember the way Daddy cried when Mama sang "Caro Nome" for him. She knew she would never understand him, ever. But she was doing the only thing she knew how to do, letting Daddy be buried right this time. The way they had buried the baby.

Thirteen . . . Fourteen . . . Seventeen. Sarah's shoulders ached. Mama pointed and down below dark figures moved into the street; people were coming out of their houses. Sarah wondered if Uncle Marsh and Keziah could hear the bells. A light or two went on.

Now it was Mama's turn. Mama was crying but she took the rope from Sarah. Her head throbbing with sound, Sarah had to put her hands over her ears. She felt the bell reverberate above her through her fingers. Even if she were deaf, she thought, she could sense the awesome sound through the liquid in her eyes, the pores of her skin, the tips of each finger. Another light went on across the street, lighting a small circular world on someone's front porch. Ring, hum, tone, ring, hum, tone. The bell throbbed into the night. Following each other like silver waves on a river, the sound expanded, pushing air in front of each ring, bouncing back at them from the sides of the mountains. The moon shone on the shoulders of the metal bell as it swung back and forth. The joyful, awful sound! *Thirty-eight . . . thirty-nine!*

"Mama. Wait!"

Sarah remembered the baby, little John Andrew. Hadn't Keziah wondered about a bell for him? Her hands still pulsated as if she had pounded something for a long time. She thought that she might die if she had to listen too long to the ringing of the bell.

"Wait!" She had to talk loudly so that Mama could hear. They were both deaf now from sound.

"Do one more for the baby," she yelled at Mama. Tears welled in her eyes and this time she let them come, didn't even blink them away.

"Both of us," Mama said. Loud, too. "We'll toll the passing bell together."

Both hands on the rope, Mama's hands over hers, Sarah pulled once again, long and slow. The bell sounded one more time, one sweet, slow peal that resounded over the town.